Ungo

11/20/2014

TO: Mary Cross,

A Beautiful a Real Woman who has a heart of Gold. Thank you for your Support. May God continue to Bless you a your Family.

Blessings,
Andrea

andrealawrence13@yahoo.com
(609) 556-7469

1

Dedication

I dedicate this book to my pain. You tried to break me but you helped me become better. The more I was afflicted the more I found myself on my knees and the stronger I became. Without you, I would never have realized how much I needed you to grow. And how much strength I had inside me to conquer you and to break totally free from you. Yes, tears of sorrow were many, but, baby, look at me now!

Aha!

One love!

Contents

Preface

In order to accept this book, you must be real with yourself. Stop making excuses for foolery. Growing up, I heard sex outside of marriage is what keeps a man. As I matured, I realized that self-respect goes so much further than a wet behind, and a slow no is always better than a fast yes.

I hope that in reading this book your heart will be mended, your soul will be healed, you embrace your true love that is already inside you, and you become whole.

I pray that God will give you strength so you will stop settling and being in denial and confront your secret demons so you can change and conquer them. Then you can move forward happy and burden free.

Remember, no one is going to love you more than you, and if he or she can't love you with your clothes on, then *keep them on*. Be strong, and love you!

Acknowledgments

Thank you, my Heavenly Father. Holy is your name. If it wasn't for you, I would not be who I am. Without you, I am nothing.

Thanks, Mom and Dad, for your love.

Thank you, Danielle R. Lawrence, my one and only sister, my best friend, for all your insights, laughter, love, countless, and priceless conversations. Now who's messing with that?

Thank you Sha-kil and Samiyah Lawrence, my lovely children. I love you both so much for your love, honesty, emotional support, and patience during our struggle. You never allowed anybody or anything to come between the genuine love that we have for each other. Thank you for believing in me even when you didn't understand and trusting the God that dwells inside me and, most of all, praying for me / with me, and doing as I say and as I do. I love you and appreciate the God in you two. My blessings.

Thank you, Pastor Andrew and Fannie Munford, my deceased grandparents, for your love and for planting the solid rock foundation of Christ in me, along with watering and cultivating it. Thank you for never judging me. Grandma, you spoke life in my desolate situation and believed God, and your faith is still in action even though you went home to glory. *Lo, your generations will reign.* Now that's some faith for ya! Granddad, your words of wisdom helped me bloom. Blessed

6

assurance, Jesus is mine. Grandma, I will bless the Lord at all times. Thank you for practicing what you preached and teaching / showing me integrity. Most of all, thank you for not being so Heavenly minded that you were no earthly good. You always kept it real.

I want to give a special shot out to my friend / Chef Patrick Fisher for everything thanks for the meetings at Starbucks and Panera Bread. Lol! I also want to thank my home-girl Alicia Emerson for being there for me. Love ya Girl!

To my spiritual sister Tanya E. Tuten. Although you are an Angel up above, I just want to thank you for making such a powerful impact in my life. Your faith was unbelievable. You always uplifted me when I was dealing with that "crazy" situation. You prayed for me and encouraged me. When it was all said and done, we went to the Chinese store and ate and laughed because we believed God. Love ya to pieces. Gone but never forgotten. Miss you much. Smile!

Thank you for the effectual, fervent prayers of the righteous that avails much from my true sisters and brothers in Christ.

Last but not least, to the author and finisher of my faith, Jesus, I thank you for relationship and not religion. Love you!

Chapter 1

Naïve

Good looks and a good shot, is a mutha.

Please don't let it delude you. Life is some *ish*. Be careful
not to let your wants supersede your needs because you will
become hoodwinked.

Yeah! I know the showered gifts and the smell of his
cologne compels you, but don't allow yourself to become open by
his smooth undertone because he might just make your sweet pink
stink and your soul so sick.

In 1994, a young suburban chick named Lisa, also known
as Twinkle is 19 , naïve, thick, pecan tan complexion with a
pretty face, beautiful smile, breasts like cannons, with a waistline
smooth and fine. Her bootie was shaped like the bottom of the
number five, and hips like whoa, while loving her ten-month-old
son to life.

At the age of eighteen, Twinkle graduated from
Willingboro High School in New Jersey and enrolled at Morris
Brown College in Atlanta, Georgia, to better herself. But she got
pregnant instead. She returned home and found a job as a certified
nursing assistant. Her parents were disappointed and embarrassed
and labeled her as rebellious.

When you live in the suburbs, there are various ideals that
you are expected to meet. The perfect family involved a mother

and father. Competition surrounded everything: who had the fanciest car, whose lawn was the best manicured, who made the most money, or whose kids went to the best college. Living in the 'burbs, doing exceptionally well is a must.

Twinkle didn't fit that criteria, nor did she want to. Frontin' was never her style. She was a what-you-see-is-what-you-get female. Either you love her or hate her. There were no in-between.

Suburban families have major problems just like every other family, but they know how to paint a perfect picture on the outside. The inside edition can be dark. The darkness came to the light for Twinkle's family when she came home with a big belly.

Twinkle's dad wasn't religious, but he was very militant and stern. He was from Opa-Locka, Florida and overcame ghetto struggles. He was determined that his family would have the best. Her father was no joke and did not take any shit from anybody.

On the contrast, Twinkle's mother was passive, naïve, and not very outspoken. She was a suburban girl raised in Trevose, Pennsylvania. She had two parents who were active Pentecostal pastors of a church in Philadelphia.

Constantly arguing with her parents, Twinkle decided to move in with her coworker Candi. Candi was also a certified nursing assistant.

Candi was not her first choice because they had different views. Candi was very sensitive and opinionated, and Twinkle was strong-willed and didn't mind telling anyone how she felt.

For example, they had a dispute in the break room during

lunch about weaves because Candi was trying to convince Twinkle to wear weaves. Twinkle told Candi no, because when she feels like wearing a weave she will.

Then Candi smacked her teeth and rolled her eyes, saying she was only trying to help her out and she was going to stay fly regardless.

Twinkle told Candi that she is not helping her out because she was fly with or without a weave.

"This right here is 100 percent human hair without the cost. So keep spending your money on that fake shit," she said. Singing to herself, "Weave in your head like mop," while nodding her head.

Candi walked away with an attitude while Twinkle continued to eat her lunch. The spat seemed to bring them closer.

However, Twinkle was angry and confused, and seeking to escape from her pain by any means necessary. So, she moved in with Candi who lived in the projects in Philadelphia, a.k.a. the Web.

The Web was full of hustlers, crackheads, baby momma drama, guys playing craps on the project steps, and a whole lot of game. Game was something Twinkle was not accustomed to because she grew up sheltered. The day she moved in with Candi, it was as if she ate from the tree of good and evil and her eyes were opened to a different world.

I am Twinkle.

Sitting on Candi's` porch one midwinter Saturday morning, I was wearing my Chanel head scarf, smoking chocolate TY and chinky - eyed. In the windowsill sat a radio playing DMX's "How's It Goin' Down." I was jammin'. I noticed a six-foot-three tall, slender, dark, handsome, bald-headed man hustling early. He looked strong and had piercing eyes. I thought of him undressing me with his eyes. I wanted him. I fell in love with his swag before he even noticed me.

After sometime, I figured out his pattern. I knew exactly what time he would be pulling up.

He's going to be mine, I thought to myself.

I began asking people about him. An around-the-way girl told me his name is Shawn, but he's called Sly.

In a Shaniqua voice, she said, "Gurl, you don't wanna mess with him 'caz he crazy. He's a woman beater. He sniffs coke. He sells drugs, and his baby ma lives right across the street.

I'm so scared of him, gurl, that if we was walking on the same sidewalk I'd cross the street 'caz I think he got some bodies under his belt."

I chuckled and responded, "You crazy." She responded, "Yeah, I am but I never killed nobody as of yet."

We high-fived each other.

"I know, that's right," but in my mind, I had to have him.

One day, my baby and only sis, Alicia a.k.a. Diamond, drove to the Web to check on her nephew and me. There is a three-year age difference between the two of us, and we are really close.

11

Shortly after I told her about the mystery man, he pulled up across the street.

"He's a bit big and mean looking," she said with a blank expression on her face.

In a seductive voice, I replied, "Yep. He doesn't know it, but he is going to be mine." Switching back to my normal tone, I said, "Come on, walk with me."

I was sharp! I had on my white Fila T-shirt, turquoise tennis skirt, and my Fila sneakers. I was feeling fly, and of course, I had Li'l Man on my hip.

"What's your name?" I asked boldly.

The short guy standing next to him answered me.

"Nut," he said.

To which I responded, "I'm not talking to you. I'm talking to the tall guy standing beside you."

So the mystery man pointed to himself and asked, "Who, me?"

"Yeah, you. I thought I was looking at you when I asked the question."

He turned around cat-eyeing me with a peculiar stare and answered, "Sly."

"That's cute, but what did your mom name you?" I replied.

"Shawn."

I asked if he was with anyone. He said no, so I gave him my number and told him to call me. After that, Diamond and I walked back to Candi's house because it was getting chilly and getting dark. I thought it was a good idea to place Li'l Man in the house with Candi's kids so they could play with each other.

Candi had three kids—a fourteen-year-old son and eleven-year-old twin girls. She was a bartender on Saturdays, and I was her babysitter. On Fridays, she watched Li'l Man if I needed her. We were always there for one another.

We rolled a blunt outside and smoked. We laughed and told jokes for the remainder of the evening and chilled. When I say Diamond is a comedian, she is not funny—she is hilarious. I promise you, after spending some time with her, your cheeks will be hurting. Not only that, you will randomly recall what she said and relive the moment again, laughing going in all by yourself.

From time to time, Sly would walk past the house. He would wave but would not approach me. I was thinking that he wasn't trying to holla because he was still messing with his baby mom. Besides, I heard that their son was only a year old.

So I remained in my bag and thought maybe he is not interested. I really wasn't beat because I already had a boyfriend who was in jail doing ten months on a parole violation. So in my mind, Sly was just a dude that was going to help me kill time before Flyez got out. Meanwhile, I was using all the money Flyez had stashed before he got locked up. I was living the glamorous life, so I thought.

Sly walked passed. "What's up?" he said in his thug voice.

"Hey," I answered in my cute but aggressive tone.

As he sat on the porch step, he asked, "What's been going

on with you?"

"Nothing. Just chillin' and waiting for you to hit me up," I answered.

"Aren't you married?" he asked.

"No," I answered. "And why do you think that?"

"Because as fine as you are," he paused, "I thought someone would of already have scooped you."

Innocently I giggled and asked, "How old are you?"

"Thirty," he blurted and quickly added. "Why, is that too old for you?"

I responded, "No. Age is just a number."

"So what you doing tonight, being that it's Friday," he asked.

"It depends what you trying to get into."

He asked me to come over his house a little later, around 9:00 p.m. and suggested we would watch movies and offered to cook for me too.

I loved to eat, especially when I get the munchies I said "okay, just call me when you're ready."

Sly had to go and take care of something but said "I could follow him to his apartment when he returned." He left, and I went inside to ask Candi if she would watch Li'l Man.

She agreed and told me, "Make sure you turn him out tonight."

"Fo' sure," I said with a wink.

Around 9:30 p.m., Sly knocked on the door. When I opened

it, he asked if I was ready. I told him yeah. He got in his car. I got in mine, and I followed him to his crib, which was literally around the corner.

I was nervous. We walked up three flights of stairs to his place. At that time, I didn't know that entering his one-bedroom apartment would lead me to the road of destruction.

His crib was clean. I sat on the couch, and he turned on the TV.

After a couple of minutes passed, I said, "I thought that you were cooking, but I don't smell any food. I thought the dinner was already prepared. Shoot! It's like 10 o'clock already and I'm hungry."

He responded that would be corny if it was already done. "I'm going to cook it now."

Rolling my eyes with a disgusted look on my face, and mumbling under my breath, "I hope this dude can cook."

Sly started cooking, and soon, it started smelling good. I rolled a blunt and helped myself to some thug passion—Alizé and Henny. I was feeling good and high, and hungry.

Finally the food was done. This guy brought me a plate with a generous helping of fried chicken wings along with a stack of southern home fries.

I hoped it was as good as it looked. Sly told me that, due to having high blood pressure, he doesn't cook with salt. So I jazzed it up with a little salt and ketchup.

"So how old are you?" I asked a second time.

Unlike earlier, this time he said he was thirty-three.

I didn't even care. I was about to get my grub on. I took a bite of the chicken. It was so good that I wanted to slap myself. The home fries were perfectly seasoned, and I didn't even need any salt. Real talk! Of course, I asked for seconds. It wasn't the time to be cute and prissy. I was hungry and was coming down off my high. The munchies were major, and good food was accessible. Shoot, it was darn near eleven o'clock, but the food was worth the wait.

After we ate, I was very relaxed, comfortable, and flirtatious. It's something how good food, a blunt, and drink can change your attitude. We were sitting on the couch hugged up and laughing. I began to feel as if I knew Sly for years.

Then the fire alarm goes off. My first instinct was to stop, drop, roll, feel the doorknob to see if it was hot, and jet.

Noticing my expression, Sly suggested that we go outside. It was January, and it was brick outside. I didn't have my coat or keys to the car. Sly saw that I was cold and went back to get our coats. Then he said, he was going to investigate and he'd be right back.

Why does it seem that the fire department takes forever to respond to alarms in the hood? It took an hour for a truck to arrive. By then, Sly had the situation under control. A woman on the second floor left a pot on the stove and was so high that she couldn't move. When the fire truck pulled up, everybody was clapping for Sly, the hero.

Back in the apartment, I was feeling I should just go

because it was so late, but Sly, my boo, had solved the problem. I was like, *Yeah he ain't no punk.* We sat down and started kissing passionately. He looked at me and asked, "Can I make love to you?"

This dude was too smooth.

"What's your first and last name?"

He couldn't say his name out fast enough.

"Do you have condoms?" I asked.

He had a jar full in the bedroom on the windowsill behind the curtain.

I was like, "Damn! You be getting it in like that?"

"It's better to be safe than sorry," he smirked.

We continued kissing. He turned off the TV and turned on "Computer Love" by Zapp. The atmosphere was set for sex. I remembered what Candi told me.

I am going to turn this man out, I said to myself.

His voice interrupted my thoughts.

"Take them off."

"What? You take them off with a li'l aggression," I insisted. "What I look like?"

Without a word, he started removing my clothes until they were all off. He entered me and gave me a feeling of pleasure that I have never experienced. He felt so good. He took his time. This big, mean-looking man was a gentle giant, so loving and so passionate. We made love a few times that night. The last time we made love, the condom came off inside of me. I was terrified, and

17

reality set in- I just met this man.

I didn't know what kind of diseases he might have. He just had a baby, and I don't want one. I went into the bathroom skizin'. I was on the toilet trying to push the condom out for about thirty minutes when Sly came into the bathroom.

"You all right?" he asked.

"No," I said. "I think I have to go the hospital."

With a look of concern, he told me to relax. "Come here. Let me get it out."

So I get up and walk into his bedroom while he is sitting down on the bed he says again let me get it out?

"I replied how are you going to do that?" While I was standing, he put his two fingers up there and pulled the condom out.

"Wow! Oh! What a night."

After that, I smoked another blunt because all that had happened was just too much to handle in one night; then I fell asleep.

This was the night the ungodly soul tie began. An ungodly soul tie is a toxic, spiritual connection that is formed, in this scenario, from sex outside of marriage, which causes you to become defiled. It fragments your soul; as a result, your mind, will, and emotions become intertwined with another person's to the point that your thoughts are not always your own as a result you become delusional. Because of this, your life is affected in a negative way. This leads you to tolerate and do things in a relationship that you would not normally do or put up with because you lustfully desire this person. Lust is a spirit that cannot be controlled because it's a desire that cannot be satisfied.

The good book says, "This I say, walk in the Spirit, and ye shall not fulfill the lust of the flesh."

When I woke up, Sly was staring at me with this look that seemed to say he didn't understand why he was feeling me the way he was.

"Good morning," he said.

"What time is it?" I asked.

"Ten thirty a.m."

"Oh shoot! My son has a doctor appointment at 11:15." I quickly washed and rinsed my mouth out and told him bye.

He asked if he was going to see me again.

"I don't know," I replied in a hurry.

Sly clinched his teeth and said, "Whatever."

I rushed home to get my son and made it to his visit. He was only going for a checkup, but I never played with missing checkups.

The next day, when I saw Sly outside, I kinda acted like I didn't see him. So he came to the porch and said, "How are you?"

Yes, this hard guy from the hood was asking me how I am. I responded nonchalantly, "Very well."

"I miss you. Can we hook up tonight," he asked.

"Maybe, are you going to cook again?"

"Yes. I'm a chef."

"Well then, I will be there."

That evening, he made steak, shrimp, broiled potatoes, and broccoli with cheese—bangin' of course—along with our blunts. And the sex was extraordinary. He would often tell me that I met my match to which I would respond, "No, you met yours."

Sometimes, we would stay in the house for days. I would call off work and he wouldn't hustle, and we would just make love, eat, and smoke. My son was at the babysitter's house during the day. The babysitter is anyone who is available at that time. You already know.

One day, I noticed that I was feeling very uncomfortable. My private area was itching, and it had a fishy odor along with a discharge. So immediately I went to the clinic, and they told me I had trichomoniasis. I was given a prescription of pills I had to take for seven to ten days. I flipped because I never had an STD.

I called Sly and indignantly asked him who was he messing with. Of course, he said nobody.

"So how in the hell did I get an STD?" I howled.

"Because you're a whore, and you were messin' with someone," he screamed back. "When I see you, I'm gonna punch you in your face."

We argued back and forth, and I hung up. Then he called me back, cussing me out, and he hung up on me. Then I called him back, cussing him out. This went on for about twenty minutes.

We didn't speak for about three months after that. I would see him around the way but would not speak. He would park across the street and visit his baby mom house for hours. I would see them walking under an umbrella in the rain, laughing and talking.

Whatever, I would think. *Flyez is coming home in forty-five days. When he gets home, we will be laughing in the rain.*

But I did miss the sex, food, and drugs with Sly. I desired him so badly. I would watch pornography often and touch myself while thinking about him, imagining that he was sexing me. I just wanted to feel his touch. I was beginning not to care that he cheated on me. I was dying inside and thought I needed his touch to feel alive again; to feel good, I thought I needed him inside me. I didn't care that he had other women. I didn't care that he was disrespectful. I needed him, and I needed it, and I needed it now!

The good book says, "For the weapons of our warfare are not carnal, but mighty through God to the pulling down of strong holds; Casting down imaginations, and every high thing that exalteth itself against the knowledge of God, and bringing into captivity every thought to the obedience of Christ."

What are imaginations? Imaginations are power-forming mental images of what is not actually present or the act of creating mental images of what has never been actually experienced. Therefore, imaginations are unreal and dreamed up. The truth is, most imaginations are lies.

Being that I was always sitting on the porch, I would always see Sly and he would always see me. One day, I made up in my mind that when I saw him next; I was going to say something

21

to him.

A few days later, I decided to walk to the Chinese store on the corner. While I was waiting for my chicken wings and fries, I heard someone's system pumping "Lady (Remix)" by D'Angelo featuring AZ. Sly walked in, cupped my face with both hands, and tongue-kissed me in front of everybody in the store.

"I miss you," he said softly, whispering in my ear. "You are the only one woman who makes me feel completely satisfied."

"I miss you too," I whispered.

Later on that evening, we made up for lost time. He had sprinkled rose petals everywhere. There were lit candles, romantic music was playing, and a bubble bath was ready. Sly bathed me and fed me grapes. He had prepared defiantly good food—chicken and shrimp alfredo. What more could a girl ask for? And the make-up sex was off the chain. For the first time, he kissed me below my navel, and it was breathtaking. He told me that he loved me. I was convinced that I was in love with him too. That night, Sly took it to another level.

I had a hood dude that could cook, clean, hustle, and still cater to my needs. He was a thug on the outside, but inside, he was a man that laughed, like to have fun, and wasn't scared to show his sensitive side.

After that wonderful night, we slept, but the sound of his beeper going off endlessly woke me up.

"Answer your pager or turn it off. I'm trying to sleep," I said grumpily.

It was his baby mom, he stated.

"I don't care who it is," I told him. "I'm here and either you are going to call her back or turn it off."

"Shut up," he yelled.

"Who are you talking to? As a matter of fact, I'm leaving," I shouted.

"When you leave, she will be here." He said, with a devious glare.

"I don't care because when I leave, everything I did to you last night, I'm going to do it to someone else, but only better."

Sly jumped up and slapped me, pulled out his pistol, and held it to my head.

"I will shoot you if you don't stop disrespecting me," he growled at me.

I yelled, "What am I supposed to say after the night we just had? Now your baby mom is blowing up your pager. How do you think I feel? I thought you loved me!"

"Get the hell outta here," he ordered.

Later that evening, Sly called and apologized. He admitted that he is insecure when it comes to me because I'm the most attractive girl he has ever been with. Sometimes he acts in ways that he doesn't mean. Of course, I went back to him.

This crazy cycle continued for four years—long after Flyez was released. I was so in love with Sly I told Flyez that it would never work out between us.

One Thursday, Sly suggested that we go to a hotel to relax on the upcoming weekend. We went to an expensive hotel for our weekend rendezvous and had a pleasurable evening, playing strip uno. Basically, we did what lovers do. We parted ways on Sunday back to the Web.

Later, I saw his car parked outside, so I walked across the street to see if I could find him. No luck. So as I returned back to my house, a guy shouted, "What's good, Jersey!"

"My name is Twinkle," I hollered back.

"You are fine. Is it possible that we can hook up?" he asked.

"No, thank you. I'm with Sly."

Then Sly appears. My smile was returned with his anger. "What did I tell you about disrespecting me?" his voice thundering.

"Babe, I was looking for you."

"That's why I'm not messing with you anymore. You're a whore. It's over," he roared.

"Whatever!" *Here we go with the shenanigans.* "Go home and smoke a blunt. I'll be there later."

When I arrived that evening, he wasn't home. But I saw him driving as I drove away. We both pulled over and got out of our vehicles.

I broke the silence. "Hey, baby."

"What did I tell you about disrespecting me?" he asked, still upset.

"I wasn't. I was looking for you, dummy," I said with an attitude.

Sly responded by punching me in my face. I walked back to my car, stunned. As I slipped the cigarette lighter in, I called him over in an innocent tone, but I planned to burn his eyes out with that lighter. As he bent down to talk to me, I shoved the hot lighter into his face. He grabbed his face while looking wall-eyed. I opened the car door, and we started rocking toe to toe.

He got scared. I believe I caught him off guard because I was not backing down. He ran back to his car.

"It's over. Don't call me anymore!" he screamed out his window as he sped away.

The nerve! He just punched me in my face, and now he is breaking up with me! Shouldn't I be the one breaking up with him?

The next day, I visited Diamond. Both of my eyes were bruised, a blood vessel in my left eye popped, my right arm looked as if someone hit me with a baseball bat, my face was swollen, and I was mad!

"Diamond, I need a gun," I said although it really was a question. "I'm going to kill him for doing this to me."

My baby sis is gangster and had all the connects. She took me to her friend Mad Dog's house in Camden, and he gave me a .45 caliber. Mad Dog said the gun had three bullets, and after I shoot Sly, I am to immediately get rid of the gun.

Next, I called my girl Bertha and asked her to ride with me to Philly so I could kill Sly. She was down. Bertha is the kind of friend who is always gleeful; nothing bothers her. She saw my beat-up face and still was smiling. Often she is in la-la land, but I loved her.

On the ride from Jersey to Philly, the .45 was in the glove compartment, Bertha was talking, but I was thinking how was I going to carry out my plan without doing time.

Finally, we pulled up in the hood. I parked and took the gun out the glove compartment.

In a panicked voice, Bertha said, "You are going to kill him for real!"

"Yes," I responded in a harsh tone. "I told you that before we left Jersey."

"I thought you were joking."

"Don't you see my face?" I asked. "Why would I joke about killing somebody?"

Now Bertha is frantic. I put the gun in my jeans and got out the car. I told her to stay put. I knew Sly was out there because I saw his car. I asked a few people if they had seen Sly. Cats are looking at my face and were saying, "Dang, sis, what happened?"

"Sly did this and when I see him, I'm going to kill him."

"You ain't going to do nothing." It was Candi's brother, Michael.

I lifted up my shirt and showed him the gun. You would have thought this guy went to law school.

"Twinkle, you crossed state line with a gun. You will spend the rest of your life in jail over him, and he is not worth it."

I didn't know how true that was, but I knew he was trying to convince me to leave.

This thug dude was darn near crying. He told me to leave and go back to Jersey with such sincerity. While he was talking, someone ran and told Sly I was looking for him and that I had a gun.

I saw Sly at a distance and yelled for him to come here. People started grabbing their kids and going inside. He didn't move. He just stood there and said nothing, trying to intimidate me. But what he didn't know, that look never scared me. Seconds seemed like minutes until he turned and walked away.

"Twinkle, let's go!" Bertha shouted in panic. That was the first time I had ever seen her frightened.

Sly started calling me at work and threatening to shoot me until he "had no more bullets left." My response was always the same. "If you were going to kill me, you would have done it that day on the street," I would say, making sure to call him punk before I hung up.

My bruises began to heal, and Sly's calls turned from hate-filled threats to attempts to elucidate himself.

"You just don't know what you've done to me," he told me. "I'm twisted. You've got me feening. I've gotta be with you. I can't sleep or function without you. You're my high, and without you I am no good."

By the same token, I couldn't let him go. All my girlfriends told me to forget him. Instead, I made excuses for him.

He loves me.

He doesn't mean to hurt me.

Sly is crazy, but so am I.

My flesh was starving, and I needed to feed it. What SWV say! "I try hard to fight it; no way can I deny it." Only Sly could satisfy that desire. I returned to him.

But the truth is our flesh is our enemy, a roaring lion looking for someone to devour; without the help of God we are out of control. Clearly most of us lack self-control because of that wild beast that dwells within.

Chapter 2
Me or Her

We had been together for four years with plenty of ups and downs, but this one threw me for a loop.

I arrived at Sly's apartment one evening. He opened the door but stopped me from entering. He said he had company.

"Who is it?" I asked.

"My friend Cedes," he answered with a frown.

Mercedes was a Spanish woman who manifested without notice.

"Who is that?" I asked.

"None of your business," he said in a seething tone. "I suggest that you leave because I'm busy."

That led to another argument.

I left the building and got into my car while Faith Evans & Mary J. Blige sang "Love Don't Live Here Anymore." A series of questions raced through my mind. *What about the love, Sly? What about the years? What about the good lovemaking? What about our pillow talks? We were soul mates. No, we are souls mates. That's what we are. And that's why there's all this drama. I was in denial thinking he's not going to stay with her because he loves me. He is just going through something.*

Every day I would sit on the porch and wait for Sly. But

when I saw him, I would grit at him and wouldn't say anything.

I would visit my friends in Jersey—Nancy also known as C, Inderea also known as Ree, Bertha, and Kimori, also known as Kay. I would tell them how much I missed him.

"I told you not to do it," C said sweetly but seriously. "You never want to listen to nobody."

"Shut up," I said. We both laughed while shaking our heads.

And then Kay said, "Straight up, get that battered bitch out your system." She hated the ground Sly walked on with a passion.

But I just could not do it.

"I know something you can do to get your mind off him," Kay said. She was a stripper and suggested that I come out and make some money.

Everybody knew I loved to dance. When I met Sly, I stopped partying because I was always with him.

Kay was petite, Japanese, black, and was bad. She attracted men and money. Her stage name was M&M because she knew all the ballers, and the ballers loved her.

So I took her up on the offer. That weekend, we drove to New York. She introduced me to all the ballers. They named me Juicy because I was thick and sexy. I was the new face in town. I discovered there that men were willing to pay a lot to have a thick, sexy girl with a pretty face who was top heavy with a flat stomach, thick hips and nice legs to dance for them. I didn't have to work hard because I was with Kay. The first night, I came home with

$700 off of lap dances. It was unbelievable. Jodeci and Raekwon's "Freakin' You" remix was pumping, along with Ice Cube – "We Be Clubbin." Dudes were giving me between $50 and $75 for a lap dance that lasted for four minutes tops. Perversion was prevalent—girls stripping while pornos was playing and ballers trying to take you home for a high price. It felt good. It felt like I was getting back at Sly in some sort of crazy way.

Kay and I were hanging tight. Basically, I was staying with her. It was fun! We were partying, dancing, drinking, smoking, and getting paid. Life was one big party. So I was a certified nursing assistant Monday through Friday. On the weekend, I was Juicy. The ballers loved the way I teased them when I danced. Why should I take all my clothes off? I wanted them to stay curious and keep coming back for me. Besides, if they couldn't see my large breast with my clothes on, they were blind.

Most of the time, the men were so drunk, high, and hurt that they would peel off hundred dollar bills just for talking to them. Nice conversation and a smile took me further than taking off my clothes. I was their fantasy girlfriend.

I learned quickly that men are looking for love in the wrong places too. They were hurting just like I was. I figured out what most women don't know. We possess the most powerful tool. It is not between our legs. It is between our ears—our brain. I didn't have to strip the majority of time. I only had to listen and talk, seductively of course, but men were drawn to me. After six months, I had regulars who told me about their baby moms, wives, kids, and jobs. I would listen, smile, and give them real advice. I was just very real with them. One thing I do know is that real recognizes real.

For my services, they would pay me between $50 and $150, depending how long we talked. I would come home with a minimum of $1,500 a night and barely had to strip. But real talk—that was God covering and protecting me because, clearly, I was in the lion's den.

The men started falling in love with me. All I did was boost their self-esteem. Instead of stroking their penis, I stroked their ego, which the majority of the time was larger of the two.

I was a strip therapist—a job that was fun, easy, and well paid. However, a greedy man brings trouble to his family. After eight months, it stopped suddenly. The manager of the club was like a father to me, but he always had his eyes on me. I would catch him staring, so I thought he wanted some although he never approached me in that way. One day he called me over.

"Juicy, why are you here? I've been watching you for months, and you are different. You're a good girl," he said. "I don't know what you're going through, but I don't want you at my club any longer."

"What?" I said in disbelief. I raised up in his face. "You can't tell me what to do."

"Juicy, this is my club, and I think you got the game twisted sweetheart. I rule this den."

"Whatever!"

"Whatever? If you come back tomorrow," he paused, "I'm not going to be so nice."

"Why are you talking to me like this? Is it because you want some?" I asked.

"Want some?" he repeated my question as if he couldn't believe I said it.

"Juicy, I have more chicks than a farm. You are one of them, but you deserve better. One day you will thank me."

I told Kay what happened. She had already gotten wind of it, but there was nothing she could do. She said as long as he's not telling me to leave I'm good.

I realized everything is not for everybody and everyone's grace level is not the same. There is a line in everyone's path that God will warn you not to cross. He will let you do you for a while, but eventually if you don't get the spiritual memo, destruction will come.

I left and never returned to the club, knowing in my heart that someone was praying for me. Still, I fell back to my old pattern of sitting on Candi's porch thinking about Sly, and now it had been about nine months since I got any. He was still with Cedes.

One day, I was driving around looking for him when I saw Mr. McGuire's van parked in front of the salon. Mr. and Mrs. McGuire were known for their banging homemade cakes and their turkey and fried chicken breast sandwiches. Mrs. McGuire cooked, and Mr. McGuire drove around the projects and surrounding area and sold the food. Their van was an upgrade of Mr. Softy because whenever you saw the van, you knew you were about to get some good food.

I parked in the salon only to find Sly's little sister, Laquita, getting her hair done. Sly always said his little sister and little brother had diarrhea at the mouth. I used that fact to my advantage.

"Hey, girl, how you been?" I asked.

"Did you hear about my brother? He beat up Mercedes. It's been about two months since they broke up, and he's been looking for you."

She explained that Sly beat Mercedes up because she was getting on his nerves, cussing him out in Spanish.

Because I changed my number and went on a sabbatical, the only way Sly could contact me was through Candi. And everybody knew that Candi was sometimey. If you caught her on the wrong day, she'd cuss you out just because.

I got my sandwich and cake and left the shop. I drove back to Candi's house and sat with her on the porch while I ate and waited. And who did I see pull up? My baby Sly.

I acted like I didn't see him of course. So he walked over.

"Can I speak to you, Twinkle?" he asked.

"Come back after I finish eating if you really want to talk," I told him.

A look of disgust crossed his face, and he walked away. I didn't care, and I wasn't scared. I always told Sly he couldn't bully a bully. I knew a side of him that nobody knew. Besides, I wanted to enjoy my food.

As Sly walked away, Candi and I were clowning him and talking crap and laughing like two old ladies.

In about an hour, he came back.

"What do you want?" I asked as I stepped off the porch.

"You."

"What about your girl," I asked.

"I don't mess with her no more," he admitted. "She was a mistake."

"You weren't saying that nine months ago, and you had a whole lot to say when she was at your place. What changed, Sly?"

He was slow to answer, so I turned to walk away. He suddenly grabbed my arm.

"I'm not that chick," I said with a dead-serious expression. "Please don't make another mistake because the outcome will be different from the last time."

I jerked my arm away from him and went to sit on the porch and poured me a glass of Courvoisier and rolled my blunt.

Before long, the liquor and marijuana got in my system, and I started feeling like I should smash Sly. It's been like nine months, so what do I have to lose? It would relieve some stress, and I'd be good for a while. Sly and I had the same appetite for sex, so I knew for sure he was coming back. Telling him off only turned him on more.

Shortly after 10:30 p.m., Sly knocked on the door. I opened the door and gave him my chinky-eyed look.

"You know what Biggie said about sex with your ex," I asked him.

"Yes," he answered, "and you're my best."

I smiled. "I'll be there in a few minutes, so drink your ginseng and smoke that dro."

He smirked and I shut the door. When I knocked on Sly's door, he opened it immediately. We started kissing and touching each other in places only lovers are allowed to touch.

"Let's take a shower," he whispered softly.

"Okay."

We had so much fun in the shower. We lathered each other, played and laughed, and enjoyed each other's wet bodies. After the shower, we rubbed one another down with some lotion, and he massaged me from head to toe. I kept saying to myself there is no place like home.

After that, he asked if I wanted my favorite ice cream sundae to which I answered, "Hell yeah!"

My favorite sundae has vanilla ice cream, wet walnuts, hot fudge, peanut butter topping, and marshmallow sauce. Of course, I'm his cherry on top. We fed each other the sundae.

In his smooth, deep voice, Sly said, "I want to do something different tonight." Jon B. "They Don't Know" played softly in the background.

"What is it, baby?"

"I want to kiss you until our lips get numb, and then hold you for the remainder of the night. We are going to be on some lovey-dovey stuff."

"What?" I thought he must have left something out. "We are just going to lay here without getting it in?"

"Baby," he said, "we have a lifetime to do that."

"What are you smoking?"

He smiled and said, "You mean more to me than that."

In my mind I was like, what's wrong with this guy? Yeah, it sounds like a good idea but just not tonight. I wondered if this chick put some roots on him and he wasn't able to get it up. All I knew is that my internal secreted compounds were throbbing like dance fever. I kept hearing in my head my girl Faith singing her song "Burnin' Up." I started singing to myself, so baby come and rescue me, I'm burnin' up. Because burnin' up I was.

We did just what Sly wanted and kissed for hours. The night was intense and made the sex that much better in the morning. After the a.m. love, Sly got up and fixed breakfast. He made scrambled eggs with cheese, cheese grits, and turkey bacon, and served it with some good old-fashioned Tropicana orange juice. Sly loved cooking, and I loved eating his food.

In my heart, we were back together. For about three months, everything was good, but one day, Mercedes visited Sly's apartment.

She was pregnant and claimed that Sly was the father.

I called Sly, and when he came home, I told him the situation and told him to go handle it. Sly insisted the baby wasn't his, but we both knew that it was.

Obviously, Sly was messing with Cedes, but I didn't care. I started to settle because the loving was good. I couldn't shake Sly's good loving.

When I asked Sly if he was messing with her, he would say no and that he didn't want her. I wanted to believe him so badly, but my gut was telling me something else. Sly finally admitted, after six months, that the baby was his.

I wondered what I was going to do but decided to stay with him. I was hurt and caught up, and my self-esteem was at ground zero. But I wasn't going to give my man up for nobody.

Sadly, Mercedes miscarried, and Sly decided to be with her in her time of mourning. So, once again, we broke up.

My pain was indescribable, unbearable. My mind kept replaying that song "You Used to Love Me" by my girl Faith Evans. When Sly left me, I didn't know what to do. I couldn't go back to the club where I was dancing. I didn't want to start fresh by going somewhere else. So I put all of my time and energy into my job and decided to go back to school part time.

Chapter 3
Grown and Sexy

I enrolled in a twelve-month computer program analyst program. A few days after I enrolled, I was terminated from my job for taking too many days off. Actually, being unemployed worked out for me. I collected unemployment, went to school full time, and spent more time with my son. I studied hard and told myself that in six months, I was going to move out of the Web and get my own spot in Jersey. I was feeling real autonomous.

I started hanging out with C, Ree, Kay, and Bertha again. On the weekends, we started taking our kids to the movies, skating rink, bowling alley, and just had fun. I needed to stay busy to keep my mind off Sly. "Our sons' ages only differ a year or two." This made the play dates so much easier. However, I still felt empty inside and I was too weak to pray for myself. So I decided to start going to my grandparent's church, which was a few minutes away from the projects and Sly's apartment. Thinking if Grandma saw me more then she would pray for me more because I was desperate for it.

My grandparents were pastors of the church. Grandma was so happy that I was coming and bringing my son to the house of the Lord.

I wasn't smoking weed as much because I wanted to become a better person not only for me but for my son as well. So I studied hard. I started reconnecting with my son by spending more time with him.

After being on unemployment for three months, I got a nice apartment in Jersey. It was a fairly new development in a glitzy town. I used my income tax return for my security deposit and paid the rent for one year. I was also able to furnish my place. It was sharp, just the way that I wanted it, with nothing lacking, except for cable. I couldn't afford it. I got local channels 3, 6, and 10. When I was lucky, I could get channel 17 and 29.

I was feeling good about myself, making As and Bs, had money—yeah, it was from the government. However, it seemed like the universe was proud of me because I was making positive changes.

Grandma often said she was proud of my accomplishments, and quoting the Old Testament book of Proverbs, she would say, "As a man thinketh in his heart, so is he." I was beginning to think and live positively. I started believing in myself and having hope. I somehow knew that everything was going to work out for the good of me and my Li'l Man. I started praying and reading my Bible and establishing a relationship with God. Instead of being on my knees in a perverse way, I was on my knees praying, calling unto Jesus knowing that he would answer. I would joke that Jesus must be black because he always comes on CP time meaning colored people. Jesus might not show up when I wanted him to, but I knew in my heart he was going to show up. Grandma would preach more often than my grandfather although he was the pastor and she was the assistant pastor. One Sunday, during my grandma's testimony, she told the whole church that I decided to leave my boyfriend and live holy unto God. She made sure that declaration was in the atmosphere whether or not I liked it. Because she was my Grandma, I had no choice but to let her get that off.

When she preached, I believed and trusted every word that came out of her mouth. She would say that I remind her of herself when she was younger. She was my grandma, but she was more like my mother. I told her everything about me and Sly. She never criticized me. She never judged me. She never told me that I was going to hell. She would only listen, laugh, and pray for me.

She would say, "Pretty girl, you have no shame and that's why God is going to use you because when you tell it, it's going to be the real deal."

I would ask, "Grandma, what do you know about the real deal?" We would laugh some more.

"Oh!" she would say, her southern accent coming through. "Grandma knows more than you think."

I simply loved her. Grandma would tell me as long as there is breath, there is always hope. She believed in the God she served and in me. Her faith was real and powerful.

In the meantime, I was still going to school. My Li'l Man was happy when I finally got cable, and my family and friends were in high spirits because I had left Sly alone. I sold my Dodge Chrysler and purchased a new red Nissan Maxima. I knew I was fly and wasn't worried about a thing. Sly would call from time to time, but I wasn't beat.

I was striving for the best because I knew God was taking care of me. I knew God was my source, and everything else was my resource. I dedicated my life to God and said the sinner's prayer. I felt so good because I had a clean slate.

I graduated with honors and started working with a mortgage company five months later. Sly called to congratulate me. He was still talking slick, but I wasn't giving in though. However, I missed him and his good food.

Eleven months went by, and I still wasn't dating. My hormones were starting to get the best of me. I was starting to feel lonely.

My spiritual development was being hindered by the lust of my flesh. My spirit was willing, but my flesh was weak, very weak. I began to crave Sly like I craved cake, and I love all kinds of cake.

Eleven long months, I was feeling crazy inside. I had been doing so well, but my flesh was getting the best of me, and my mind was not my own. I lost control and needed Sly just one more time. I was feeling like the song "My Body" by LSG.

This ungodly soul tie was keeping me in bondage, but I started to make excuses for myself.

Hell, I'm grown! I just finished school; I got my own place, so why can't I get some. Shoot, I deserve it! I called Sly.

"When are you going to come see my new place?" I asked, adding that I would cook for him. I learned to cook a little bit in the time we had been apart.

"Twinkle, I don't want no trouble over Jersey."

"The only thing that is going to be in trouble is the bed headboard," I replied.

He laughed and said, "Oh really!"

"So what do you think, Sly?"

A bit suspicious, he asked, "You not going to put any rat poison in my food are you?"

I sighed deeply. "Sly, you eat with nasty crackheads." Then instantly changed up and said, "No, you don't. I just remembered, they don't eat. Are you coming or not?" I said irritably.

Sly replied, "I can't stand you and your smart-ass mouth."

"Whatever! I can't stand yours either," I shot back.

In the end, we decided that Sly would come for the entire weekend. It was Tuesday, and I spent the rest of the week thinking of how many ways I was going to love him, thanks to Ms. Toni Braxton. I was going to be Sly's weekend lover.

Come Friday, C watched Li'l Man until Sunday. Of all my friends, she remained neutral when it came to Sly. She just wanted me to be happy.

I planned on making the weekend worthwhile for Sly. At this point, he and I had been off and on for about five and a half years.

He called to tell me he was on his way and made sure he had the correct directions.

I told him to follow the white lines and the green signs, and he'd get here. "It's really not that hard, Sly, reading is fundamental."

My anticipation level was sky high. I had scented candles burning and was playing "No Other Love" by Faith Evans. I was wearing black lingerie with red pumps, smelling edible—yeah, good to eat. My eyes were outlined perfectly, my nails, feet and hair were done, and my lips were glazing like satin.

I approved of the image of sexual seduction that gazed at me from the living room mirror and practiced sexy facial expressions.

Around 8:30 p.m., the doorbell rang. I looked out the peephole to see my baby Sly. I opened the door with such joy and thought this day, April 16, is going to be a day I will always remember.

Sly was holding three dozen red roses, two cards, and a Snickers bar, along with a Sprite. Four big grocery bags were on the ground. We greeted each other with a kiss, and he told me that I looked as sexy as ever.

I told him to come in. He did and gave me everything that was in his hands, and then went back to get the grocery bags.

"What's in the bags?"

He answered, "If you help me put the food up, then you will see."

"Sly, really. What, you think you got brass balls now because you are here? Ugh!"

"You know your greedy ass want to know."

I smiled, thinking my honey is officially back.

He put the bags on the kitchen table and started removing the groceries—two big bags of colossal shrimp, four porterhouse steaks, a large bag of broccoli, sharp cheddar cheese, four cheese DiGiorno pizza, fish sticks, fries, a dozen eggs, turkey bacon, waffles, Klondike bars, ice cream, whipped cream, fruit snacks, cereal, and to drink, Little Hugs, and his favorite, Ocean Spray cranberry juice.

"Babe, I thought you were cooking," he said.

"I am. I was waiting for you to get here. Don't you think it would be corny to already have the food fixed?"

"No," he answered. "You are not a chef like me."

"Well, I didn't want you to think that I put poison in it. But since you are here with your porterhouse steaks, you can do what you do. I'm not going to stop you."

Sly replied, "I can't stand you."

"The feeling is mutual."

"Where is Li'l Man?"

I told him that he was with C this weekend.

"Oh, I bought him some books, games for his Game Boy and a few Polo outfits along with some T-shirts. I was going to surprise him and take him to the park. I really miss that li'l dude and think about him often."

"When are you going to start cooking?"

"Since you brought the food over, you may as well cook."

"I knew it," Sly replied.

"Well, make yourself at home," I said as I went into the bedroom to watch TV.

Before long, Sly called me. "Twinkle, come here?"

I asked, "For what?"

"Tonight we are going to do something different."

"This dude always wants to do something different," I mumbled out loud. "That's his problem."

"You're gonna watch me cook," Sly continued, "Because you need to learn."

"What do you think I've been doing for the past eleven months," I asked as I returned to the kitchen.

He looked at me and said, "Well, help me."

"Are you serious?"

"Yes, Twinkle. Stop being lazy because you were supposed to cook anyway."

Sly had me clean the shrimp and peel them. He had me take the little vein out too. Who does that? Then I had to season them. Then he fussed about me putting too much Old Bay on the shrimp.

"That's why you should have done this yourself. Because you are too damn particular," I said with a grunt.

He told me to be quiet and stop acting like a baby.

"Negro, this is my house, and I can act any way I choose to. If you don't like it, there is the door, boo."

"Boo these nuts," he told me.

"Whatever!"

We both laughed. Dinner was starting to smell right, and

we were sipping on sangria and, of course, smoking while watching TV in the living room. Sly wanted me close to him.

When dinner was finally ready, Sly fixed my plate, which he called the "fat momma's plate," and we sat on the floor Japanese style. I don't know what made Sly bring chopsticks over, but, hey, if he liked it, I loved it. I just was happy that I wasn't alone anymore. My honey was home, and I had a honey do list prepared.

Sly didn't mind cooking, organizing my cabinets, cleaning, sewing, or fixing things. He could figure out how to do anything and never complain. For me, having him cook and wash dishes was a form of foreplay.

Yes, this man did chores and did them well. Between me and you, I thought he had a touch of obsessive-compulsive disorder, but it worked for me. When Sly was around, I didn't have to do anything. I was in love with him.

After dinner, he told me to open my cards. The first one was a tearjerker. It read something like:

I'm sorry for all of the wrong I've done to you and I never meant to hurt you, and I realized that I became a better person when I met you.

There was $1,100 in that card. The second one was an I-love-you card with no money in it. You know that I was looking for some more money it read something like:

There is not enough money in the world to buy your love.
Love,
Sly

While I was reading the cards, "Touch Me, Tease Me" by Case and Foxy Brown was playing. I was overjoyed.

Sly told me the cards and money was his peace offering because he felt so penitent, and he wanted to stay in my good graces. I told him as long as he didn't start acting hundred - faced he would.

"It's a clear, blue day, and the plane has landed," I told him. "Please don't depart again."

He promised me he would never leave me again and apologized for all of the hurt he put my son and me through. He said he knew I was strong. He called me a thoroughbred. He said I am his baby because unlike the other women he dealt with; I work, pay my bills, and take good care of my son.

"Thank you, VP." Vanilla pound cake, that's the nickname he gave me because I am sweet and thick and that's his favorite cake.

"I'm sweeter than ever," I told him. "Come and see."

"You starting early."

"Yeah, because you're here."

Sly said, "I missed my VP. I haven't felt this way since we

broke up. I'm scared because I don't understand why I love you like I do. You know, I gave you my innocence."

With that, I said, "Okay, Sly, you about to mess up the mood. Dude, you are fourteen years older than me. You didn't give me your innocence because you were never innocent. Tell that bullshit to what's-her-name."

"One thing that hasn't changed for sure is your smart-ass mouth," he said. "Your mouth is a gift to piss people off."

"Your gift is to make people believe your lying ass," I giggled. "You're in the wrong profession. You should become a lawyer because most lawyers are paid liars. If you can deal with crack heads, surely you can deal with a staff."

We laughed, and he jokingly said, "Get out of here."

"You know that I'm telling you the truth."

Sly pulled me close and whispered, "The truth is that I want you and I miss you."

"I want you too." The music switched to "Feenin'" by Jodeci. We started kissing slowly. He moved to my neck, sucking and kissing. I started to feel him down below. He sure wanted me. My temperature started rising. We kissed for about thirty minutes. I began to hear this slow, intense paradiddles in my head. I was ready to enjoy this limo ride. So I got on top of him. As I felt him, I started moving back and forth slowly to the rhythm of the music. We drove each other for about an hour. The ride was hot and sweaty and so good.

As we started to get closer to our final destination, the ride became harder and faster, harder and faster, harder and faster. Sly grabbed me and held me real tight as we reached our final destination together.

He moaned, "I will never let you go. Have my baby."

"Baby?"

"Yes. You are my wife, and nobody will ever come before you. Promise me that you will never let me go."

Tears welled up in my eyes. My honey really loves me.

Sly felt so good. *And I made my heart believe that he is good.*

Chapter 4
Lost and Turned Out

I was turned out. I told Sly I would have ten of his babies, though I knew he had seven kids by seven different women already. I didn't care. He was my man; we had history together. We weathered the storms and, somehow, someway, reconnected with one another no matter what. We would just begin where we left off. I knew this time it was real. Nobody couldn't tell me differently. I knew he loved me and that none of his other women compared.

I was that girl, Twinkle. I was whole again, and my honey was back. Sly and I were getting along really well, no drama. We were doing what grown people do.

He would celebrate the big 40 in June. I wanted to do something really special for him. I decided to take him on a weekend getaway.

Because I really enjoyed my job, I was not trying to jeopardize it by taking off during the week. At the end of the day, there was nothing going on but the rent.

I planned for us to go to the Poconos. Sly didn't know where we were going. I just told him that we were going out of town. We left on Friday evening, and he drove his black Lexus. I directed him on how to get there. We arrived, and it was time for the fun to begin.

We got into the champagne glass tub and acted like two teenagers in love.

I noticed he was distant like he had something else on his mind.

"Are you all right?" I asked him.

"Yeah."

We went horseback riding and canoeing. Then we took a nature walk. We did a lot of talking and kissing. It was a fun-filled weekend, but I felt like Sly was hiding something with his kisses. I just couldn't pinpoint what.

On our way back to Jersey, he said, "Babe, when we get home, I can't stay the night."

"Why, Sly?" I asked without trying to hide my frustration.

He said his brother had plans to celebrate his birthday with him. Deep in my heart, I knew something wasn't right. It just wasn't sitting right with me.

When we returned to my apartment, he quickly helped me with my luggage.

"You must really be in a rush to hang out with your brother."

"No, baby, stop acting like that. I'll see you on Wednesday," and gave me another kiss.

"Be good, baby," I said as he walked away.

I figured he would call me Monday morning to tell me to have a good day before I go to work like he always does. Monday I would feel better. But I woke up Monday to the alarm clock, not Sly's morning call. Sly always called before my alarm would go off. The alarm was our cue to hang up so I wouldn't be late for work.

I called Sly. The voicemail picked up. I called back again and again. It kept going to voicemail. I decided to drive to Philly—I rationalized—to make sure everything was okay with him. I was nervous when I knocked on the door because part of me believed he had someone in there. I just knew he did, and that's why he wasn't picking up his damn phone.

Sly answered the door fully clothed. It was 8:00 a.m. I walked in, looking around suspiciously.

"Honey, why didn't you call me like you normally do?"

Agitated, Sly replied, "Because I just left you yesterday."

"So what," I screamed. "You always call me in the morning."

"Twinkle, stop questioning me."

"You must have forgotten who I am. I will question God, you, and anybody else I choose to."

He sat down on his couch, and I noticed a passion mark on his neck.

"Sly, who put that passion mark on you?"

"You did."

"No, I didn't." Then I noticed he had two passion marks on both sides of his neck. I almost believed that I might have put one there, but not four.

"Who in the hell put these passion marks on your neck," I said, yelling this time.

"Twinkle, you are messing with my high, and it's too early for this."

I shouted, "Sly, you just left me last night—not even within twenty-four hours—and now you have passion marks on your neck."

"I don't even know what you're talking about right now, and I'm not going to argue with you."

"Okay, Sly," I said and left because I had to get to work.

After work, I went to Sly's brother's barbershop, which happened to be next to Sly's apartment.

I asked his brother, Thomas, also known as BM for Big Mouth, if he had seen Sly.

"Yeah, Twinkle. Your boy Sly is with Julius," he responded.

"Julius? The pimp?"

Now everybody in the Web knew about Julius and how he pimped tricks. The Web was a place where everybody knew everything about everybody. That's just how it was.

Julius was a sharp OG. He was around sixty-five and had lip game for days. He was still telling his tricks on the avenue to go fetch. He would come in the barbershop from time to time to get his haircut and be red carpet sharp.

BM was quaint, and we were cool, I think, because of me being around for so many years with Sly. We established this big bro-li'l sis bond. He would often ask me why was I with his brother. He'd call Sly cheap. He'd say his brother has a sex problem and all the women he messes with are big Zs. Z is for zilch/zeros.

He suggested that when Sly cheats on me, I shouldn't cry because those girls are not worth my tears and neither is Sly. BM would tell me that I deserve a man who would buy me furs and diamonds and take me on expensive trips. I belong on his calendar because I'm a fly girl.

He went on to say, "The problem with you, Twinkle, is that you are always giving my brother dessert first. When it's time for him to eat dinner, his appetite is spoiled."

"What?" I asked.

"Twinkle, you are a little slow."

"Well then, speed me up," I said, "since you running your mouth a mile a minute."

"Twinkle, you need to get sharper. Monogamy is a full course meal, and the dessert is the loving. But because you are always spoiling my brother, he has no appetite for dinner. You are doing it wrong, sis. I'm sure your mom taught you not to eat dessert before your dinner because it will spoil your appetite."

I nodded my head in agreement.

"Well, listen to me. Do it right and both parties will be jolly and full, and nobody's stomach will be upset."

BM reminded me of the old saying about why buy the cow if you're getting the milk for free. It's funny how someone else can recognize your worth when you cannot.

BM was a good dude, but he was a product of his environment. I respected him and loved him to the utmost.

Changing the subject, I asked, "So why is Sly with Julius?"

"Because he's a pimp," BM answered bluntly.

"A pimp! Since when?"

"For about three months."

"BM, are you lying?" I couldn't believe what he was saying.

"Twinkle, I swear on my son's tattoo." He pointed to his left forearm. Now smiling from ear to ear BM said, "We live by the pussy and we die from the pussy."

My heart dropped.

"Twinkle, my brother's sex problem is serious, and when he was in jail, he wore a skirt," he added jokingly. "For the life of me, I don't even know why he is pimpin' chicks. From what I hear, you and him go at it like rabbits daily. He says you satisfy him on a whole 'nother level. He says you are super fresh just like the grocery store, and there is nothing lacking with you and him."

I replied, "Honesty and loyalty is what's lacking."

So I asked BM if he knew who put the passion marks on Sly. He explained how Julius threw a party for Sly, and Julius's girls put them on him. He called them the passion mark hookers.

So basically, Sly rushed off Sunday night to go to an orgy. My pain and disbelief were so great that I went home and cried. Why would Sly risk contracting AIDS by sleeping with hookers?

Why would he risk his life—furthermore my life?

I remember learning in health class that when you have sex with someone, you are having sex with everyone they had sex with for the last seven years and everyone they and their partners have had sex with for the last seven years.

I was certain Sly was using again. I could tell by his irritable moods and lack of money. He still had money, but his bankroll was real weak.

I called Sly a million times and left a million messages, but he didn't return my calls. So I drove over to his apartment. He didn't answer his door. I wrote a note in which I cussed him out and slipped it under the door.

As I walked away, I thought, *this paphian guy is grimy, and he thinks it's normal.* This dude is sick. He doesn't give a damn about me. To him, I am just a good, wet ass - some in-house pussy. A Jersey girl, with a good job, a place, fly, holding my own, 14 years younger than him – I made Sly look good. I was something to brag about to his boys. I was young and restless. I had energy to chase him and didn't care how foolish I looked doing it. Through all the hurt, I kept saying Sly is my man and I'm not going to give him to nobody, not by any means.

I called Kay. She told me to restrict myself from Sly and to screw anybody but him. I couldn't. I tried to, wanted to, but something inside of me had to have Sly. Whatever it was, it was driving me insane. I was madly in love with Sly. Although I knew he was community dick, I did not care. I was lost and turned out just like how the Whispers used to sing. Instead of Olivia it was Twinkle.

I started smoking weed more than usual to try to forget Sly. I also stopped paying my bills on time. As a result, my cable was disconnected.

C, Bertha, Ree, and Kay all urged me to forget him. My sister was constantly analyzing the situation. She always made me feel better, but the pain was still devastating.

Then one evening, Sly showed up unannounced. I knew it was him and didn't want to answer, but this strong desire took over. He had a measly $50, some salmon and lobster. He told me he was sorry, and he wanted to cook a seafood dinner.

"Who you pimpin', Sly."

He told me nobody and his brother just told me that.

"Why in the hell," I yelled, "would someone just say that?"

Sly didn't respond.

"Oh! Now the cat got your tongue. You real quiet, Sly. We know you always have something to say. So who is she?" I demanded.

In a straightforward manner, he answered, "I have sex with other women just to manipulate them for my own pleasure, but it's nothing personal against you. You shouldn't take it personal. It's quantity with those chicks I wipe my dick off, and I leave, but with you, baby, it's quality."

"That's supposed to make me feel better? If I start having sex with other dudes, would you still be here?"

Sly responded, "No, because there would be no need for me."

"That's the way I feel. There is no need for us. So leave, Sly."

Sly said, "Baby, I'm just telling you the truth and keeping it real with you. See, if I lied to you and was sneaking, then you would be mad about that too. I can't win with you. I'm always between a rock and a hard place with you."

"Yeah, your place is always hard and that's your problem. "Now," my voice rose to a scream, "get the hell out my house!"

Sly left, and I cooked the salmon for dinner. My son and I went to bed around 9:00 p.m.

A sound at my bedroom window woke me around 12:30 a.m. It was Sly throwing pebbles. I had turned off my phone so he couldn't reach me that way, and the fan was running, so I couldn't hear the doorbell.

"Go back to those whores and leave me alone," I shouted as I opened the window.

"I don't want them," he said. "I'm here trying to make up with you, but you keep quitting me."

"This is not the time. Unlike you, I have to go to work tomorrow. Go home."

"This is home," he responded. "Open the door, VP."

After going back and forth for a few minutes, I told him, "Yeah, you are here, but we are not having sex. In fact, I'm going back to bed—alone."

"VP, take a shower with me," he asked. "I've been throwing rocks out here for about an hour, and it is the middle of August, I'm sweaty and need to relax."

I said, "Ain't nobody ask you to stand outside for hours and throw rocks like we are the upgrade Romeo and Juliet couple. Man, get out of my face."

"Will you please take a shower with me, VP?"

His begging worked. When we got in the shower together, and what a surprise! There was a passion mark on his back.

Okay, let's be real here. We all know that there's not that much passion between a man and a woman. Women don't get off by humping a man's ass. So my question is, who was playing in Sasha's—oops—I mean, Sly's, ass. Did he really think that I didn't peep the Sodom and Gomorrah secret shade? BM wasn't lying about Sly wearing a skirt when he was locked up, now was he? I didn't want to believe that my man was someone else's man too. So I put on the honey blonde wig and went straight into denial.

I didn't let on that I had seen it. I just got out and went to bed.

Pain engulfed me. I let Sly into my heart, and I allowed him to break my heart into small pieces. It was another reminder that he didn't love me nor did he love himself. He was clearly confused, and so was I.

He tried to hug me, but I told him to leave me alone in my Annie Wilkes tone from the movie *Misery*. And miserable I was.

After I woke up, Sly asked me what was wrong.

I told him that he is what's wrong with me. "I'm tired of all the lies, the women, the manipulation, and the deceit."

"Baby, it's too early for this," Sly complained.

Forcefully I responded, "Is it? Because it's never too early for your dick to get hard. It's never too early for you to lie in my face, but now, since I'm checkin' you, it's too early? No, it ain't too early. It's just too early for you to face reality and for you to take responsibility. It's too early for you to get a job. Unless you leave, I'm going to continue to go off on you. So get your black ass out my queen-size bed and leave now."

Sly was angry. He called me all types of dumb bitches and hoes while he put his clothes on, then stormed out the door.

I didn't even care. I yelled after him, "Mother had you. Mother f@#$ you."

Then I got dressed and went to work.

Chapter 5

Ain't Beat

Life goes on. I wasn't beat, or so I thought. However, I continued to smoke weed and masturbate—something I knew how to do oh so well. But this was my life. I definitely was playing that CD by Mary J.

Now I'm twenty-five, about to turn twenty-six. It's November, and Sly is on his disappearing acts. I started to get used to them and wasn't fazed like before.

I returned to church. Through all my sin, hurt, anger, perverseness, and low self-esteem, Grandma always saw my beauty and always loved me. She continued telling me, "Pretty girl, you will make it."

I didn't really feel beautiful. I felt like I was existing, not living. I realized that I was using weed for my mental pain medicine and watching pornos to fantasize about Sly for my physical gratification. But as the old song goes, "Ain't nothing like the real thing, baby."

Sly continued to call me. I would ignore his phone calls, and he would leave nasty messages saying his favorite names for me, "You bitch" and "Whore."

I would listen to the messages and say, "Right back at cha, punk!"

He was so predictable with his split personalities. One

minute, he loves me, and everything is good in the neighborhood, then within less than thirty seconds, I'm a bitch and a whore. I considered him to be unstable and allowed him to make me the same way. When he was up, I was up. When he was down, I was down.

Eventually, I got to the point where I was happy with myself and reasoned that Sly could be irrational by his damn self.

One day, I decided to visit Candi. A group of guys was on the porch doing what they do—sharing the latest gossip. Candi was sipping on some Courvoisier as I took a seat on the porch.

Candi said whenever Sly saw her on the porch; he would ear-beat her concerning me. Just to get him to leave her alone, she would lie and say she would call me. Candi hated Sly's alimentary canal.

She is eleven years older than me, was born and raised in the hood. They say the hood has two types of females—ghetto bunnies and gutter rats. Candi was considered a ghetto bunny because she was sharp and had a decent shop.

"Straight up, I know that Sly shot is all that but stop putting all of your marbles in one basket because it's too many men out here," she told me to forget Sly. "He ain't shit and never gonna be. Sly's a nasty-ass fly, and every time he lands on you, he regurgitates. He's just nasty, and you can do so much better than him. Wake the hell up, Twinkle. Stop acting like a bimbo."

I responded, "You wake the hell up, Candi. You have a plethora of dicks running up inside of you, so what does that make you?"

In her loud, raspy voice, she replied, "You damn skippy jack. I'm a high-priced hoe. That's why I have ninety-nine problems, and dick sure ain't one."

We just started laughing.

"Furthermore," Candi interrupted the laughter with one more point about Sly, "after Sly left my porch, he walked right across the street to his baby mom's house. That's why I didn't bother to tell you."

Still, the thought of cheating on Sly never sat right with me. Oftentimes, I would think of all the things he did for me, and say to myself I know Sly loves me. Clearly, I was delusional.

I asked Candi, "Do you think another guy is going to cook for me, serve me breakfast in bed? Do you think another man is going to dance with me for hours and then rub my feet?"

"Damn," said Candi, "Sly do all that?"

"Yes, and a lot more."

"I see why you lost and turned out."

"I'm not lost and turned out, but I'm spoiled." Sly knows all of my soft spots. A new dude would have to learn, and I don't have time to teach another man," I rationalized. "And I'm definitely not cooking for another man. The only man I will be cooking for is Li'l Man. When Sly cooks, he fixes my plate and serves me. He knows my favorite snacks and my favorite ice cream sundae. I'm going to wait for Sly to change. I know he will. I know he will."

It's funny how hope sometimes can be paralyzing and keep you in bondage.

"Okay, Twinkle, you wait and I'll date. Look, we just talked his black ass up."

I took his sudden appearance as a sign that he would one day do right by me. Sly walked toward the porch, and I went to meet him halfway. I wanted to jump into his arms, but I played it cool.

"You still mad?" he asked.

"Maybe," I said.

"Do you miss me?"

"A little bit," I replied, and then asked him if he missed me.

"I wouldn't be standing here if I didn't. How long have you've been out here?"

"For about two hours," I answered.

He asked, "You'll be having a birthday soon, right?"

"You tell me."

"I can't stand your mouth."

I said, "Then why are you still standing here?"

"You are such a suburban girl with ghetto ways."

"That's why you love me and be ear-beating Candi about me. You're a geek on the inside. You got the whole hood fooled, but not your girl Twinkle."

"Twinkle, can you be my star because I've been wondering where you are," said Sly as he held my hand.

I replied, "That's what I'm talking about right there. Who says that?"

We both snickered.

"I knew you were coming out here today," Sly responded.

"Oh really! How did you know?"

"I can feel you just like you can feel me. You're not the only one with psychic ability."

"Shut up," I told him while sucking my teeth.

Then Sly brushed my chin gently with is fingers and said, "You are so beautiful."

Just like that, he went from acting childlike to being old school. He had me thinking about "You Are So Beautiful to Me," by Ray Charles.

"Thank you," I smiled.

Then Sly said, "Let's go to Jersey where there are trees, landscaped yards, fresh air, peace, and where the white folks walk with their dogs and cats."

"Boy, you are so stupid. You know you are something else," I said as I shook my head and smiled.

Shouting over my shoulder to Candi, "I'll talk to you later."

She yelled back, "Remember what I told you."

I chuckled.

When we got to my apartment, Sly asked, "What did you cook?"

"Nothing." Li'l Man is with his aunt Diamond so there was no reason for me to cook.

Sly went straight to the kitchen.

Digging in the freezer, he asked, "Who cooked the salmon?"

"Me," I responded.

"Who taught you how to cook it," he asked.

"Why do you want to know?"

"Are you hungry," he asked

"If you're cooking," I said, "yes!"

"You have waffles and chicken in here," said Sly.

"I know."

"Well, that's what we are eating tonight."

"That don't even go together," I told him.

Sly said, "Trust me. This stuff right here is mean. Believe your honey."

"Okay, Sly."

We ate fried chicken and waffles. It was so so so good. We talked and kissed, but his kisses didn't feel the same. It felt like he didn't want to kiss me, like he was forcing himself to kiss me. It was a weird feeling.

However, we still made love. It was corny. I pretended to enjoy it, but I couldn't wait until it was over. I thought I was tripping because we haven't been together in a while.

I called Kay the next day because I was confused.

"Twinkle, it seems to me that your body is rejecting him," she said.

"Rejecting? Sly? My body never rejected him."

Kay responded, "Well, there's a first time for everything, and it's about time."

The thought of my body rejecting Sly's love after six years was unbelievable. I'm just going through something. I used to feel stress-free, but now the act felt burdened. When Sly released inside of me, I felt as if all of his crazy issues were coming in me. I think Sly knew that something wasn't right but couldn't put his finger on it either.

I forced myself to make love to Sly because if I didn't, he was going to get it from somebody else, but the reality was, he was always sexing someone else.

Afterward, I felt sick so I made an appointment with my doctor. I was pregnant.

I said to myself this is a fine time to be pregnant.

Two weeks later, I told Sly. He was ecstatic. I was surprised by his positive reaction. He said he wanted a little girl because he wants me to know how he feels when I get smart with him.

"Well, if we do have a daughter, she will not be getting smart with me. If anything, she will be getting smart with you because you don't believe in discipline. The joke's on you, Sly. You are about to get a run for your money."

We laughed.

I requested a follow-up doctor's visit because of the discomfort during intercourse. My doctor had failed to test me for

STDs and HIV/AIDS previously, so the tests were done at this visit.

My doctor said if anything was found, there were ways to prevent STDs and viruses from spreading to the baby. I was so scared. Though I knew Sly was having unprotected sex, I also knew he had an HIV/AIDS test every summer.

I never knew the true reason why, but when I would ask him, he would say that was something he would do every summer along with not drinking alcohol for a week to clean out his system. When his results came back, he would be so relieved and tell everyone he was negative.

November 30 was a good day. The sun was bright. I woke up to two of my favorite men, breakfast in bed, and a whole bunch of balloons. It was my birthday.

Sly bought me a lemon cake from Mrs. McGuire and a bad Kolinsky mink coat with my name engraved inside. It was a perfect fit. Li'l Man got me some smell goods and the cutest card with $5 in it.

"I picked everything out myself," he boasted. I smiled. "Thank you, baby." I gave him a big hug.

That evening, Sly took me to dinner and a movie. The entire day was enjoyable. When we got back to my place, we watched some TV and eventually went to bed. Sly held me close and said he couldn't believe I was nineteen years old when he met me.

I interrupted, "And I'm still young."

We talked about the baby. He said he was thinking of marrying me. I thought the movie must have made him sentimental.

Sly began to kiss me, but something still wasn't right. Each kiss felt like he was saying I'm sorry. *Sorry for what?* I questioned. What is he hiding?

After being with someone for so long, you start to understand the language of their heart. People know how to say things that are appealing to your ears, but they don't mean what they say. It's for their own personal gain.

The Bible instructs us to be as harmless as a dove and as wise as a serpent. I'm not sure about the harmless part, but you must be wise for sure.

The next morning, Sly went home to hustle, and I called off work because I wasn't feeling well. The doctor's office called me that afternoon. The nurse stated she had good news. I was negative for HIV/AIDS. She also had bad news. I was positive for chlamydia. I needed to come in as soon as possible to get a prescription, and my child's father needed to be treated.

I hung up the phone and cried, thinking back when Sly gave me trich. Now, six years later, this shit.

This explains the sorry-ass kisses. An hour passed before I finished crying. I called Sly. Of course, he didn't pick up his phone. I called again, and he still didn't answer. I decided to drive to Philly and tell him face-to-face.

Chapter 6
Psychotic

I covered the peephole and knocked on the door. When he asked who was it, I disguised my voice and said Monique.

He opened the door with just his draws on. I saw a significant brownish spot around his crotch. It looked as if I interrupted him while he was smashing a chick that had some type of STD. It was so disgusting.

I yelled, "What is that shit on your underwear?"

Sly started talking and acting crazy. He pulled out his diseased dictonite. Some might call it that kryptonite. Sly had the balls to say, "This belongs to you."

He was looking back and forth as if he was hearing voices.

"What are you smoking?" I asked and started cussing him out. "Oh, this is the reason why you were in a rush to leave—so you can smash a diseased chick."

Sly was so high he didn't know what to say. He slammed the door in my face.

Here I am, pregnant with his baby, and he has a diseased chick inside his apartment, and he has the nerve to slam the door in my face.

I banged on his door and warned him that if he didn't open it, I was going to kick it down. He didn't open it, so I started kicking. On the seventh kick, the door flew off the hinges. I ran into his bedroom. The radio was loud. It sounded like they were listening to "I Hate You So Much" by Kelis, and that's how I felt. I saw this monstrous chick riding Sly like she was the lone ranger. His draws were still on. He was blindfolded and his mouth was wide opened. His mouth appeared to be a black hole as if he had eaten black licorice, and his mouth was foaming.

On the dresser I saw crack, a crack pipe, and ecstasy pills. The chick had a scary, blank stare on her face and was panting like a crazed hyena. She was spinning her head in a circular motion as if she was demon possessed. Her hair was a dirty blonde; dirty like it had not been washed for months. The two of them were so high they didn't realize I was in the room.

I snapped. I grabbed the chick by her hair and punched her in her face repeatedly. I tried to break her face. She fell off Sly. He removed the blindfold and sat there like he was frozen. I jumped on the bed and kicked him in the balls like I was playing kickball.

He shouted, "I'm sorry! I'm sorry!"

I then jumped off the bed like I was a ninja and ran into the kitchen. I came back into the bedroom with a kitchen chair and bashed Sly upside his head. The chair broke. Blood was everywhere. The girl caught my attention as she tried to get up. I took the broken chair, hit her with it, then sprayed her with Mace. I spit on the both of them and ran out the apartment building like a maniac.

I drove back to New Jersey doing 115 miles per hour

listening to Guns N' Roses's "Welcome to the Jungle" and went straight to Kay's house. I told her what happened. She was stunned. I told her I had enough of Sly's shit.

"This time, I'm really going to kill him."

Kay said something about me calming down because of the baby.

"I don't care," I screamed as I left her house outraged.

I paced the floor at my place for about an hour. Sly called.

"Bitch," he yelled into the phone, "when I see you I'm going to kill you."

"We'll see, bitch ass," I said then hung up without giving him a chance to respond.

I grabbed the fur coat Sly gave me and drove back to Kay's house, taking note of a dead possum on the street. Kay never locked her door, so I walked inside and demanded a knife, a clear plastic bag, and some plastic gloves.

Kay had knife collections that once belong to her Japanese grandfather. She had all kinds of swords, machetes, and survival knives.

"What do you think you are going to do?" Kay asked.

"Kill him! Duh!"

"It always amazes me that even in your anger you still have jokes," she said.

"Kay, I am so serious right now."

"I know," she said. "That's why this is so funny."

Kay was off the chain and got out her sharpest survival

knife and tested its sharpness by licking her finger and touched the point of the knife.

"Yeah, this it," she assured.

Then Kay went into her pantry and came back with a clear plastic bag and yellow cleaning gloves.

"I'll talk to you later," I told Kay. "Right now, I'm on a mission."

I drove back to the spot where I saw the possum. With the gloves on, I picked up the road kill by its tail and put it in the plastic bag. It must have weighed about thirty pounds.

I was thinking what I would say if someone stopped to ask me what I was doing. It was broad daylight after all. I decided that I would say I am a college student and my class is dissecting road kill for extra credit.

But, oh my god! There were flies swarming everywhere, and the possum's eyes were looking right at me eerily. It was gruesome. Its guts were hanging out, and it smelled worse than one hundred dead fishes and a chicken coop together.

Words can't describe what I felt as I drove back to Philly with a dead possum on the front seat of my car. The thing was reeking so bad that I continued gagging during the drive. However the smell didn't stop me from bumpin' my system up all the way down there to Black Rob "Like Whoa," and Noreaga's "Super Thug." I had it on repeat. "What! What! What! What!" Because that's how I was feeling. Like Whoa!

My intention was to show Sly what death looks like and to

let him know he was going to be next. All this was the warning before the destruction. When I pulled up in front of his apartment, Sly's brother, BM, was standing outside. When he saw the gloves, he asked, "What did you do to my brother?"

I shouted, "Nothing yet."

I ran up the stairs carrying the mink coat and the possum. There was no door to Sly's apartment, and no one was home.

I walked right in and spread the mink over his bed and wrapped it around the dead possum. I placed a note on top that read, "This is what something dead looks and smells like. You're next! Signed, You Know Who."

When Sly un-wrapped the gift, he would see the possum through the clear bag.

I drove through the projects to see if I could find Sly. I told everybody what I had done and they laughed. They couldn't believe it. You know, the majority of the people in the projects are crazy anyway. I fit right on in.

I was looking deranged. My wig was lopsided. I didn't even brush it. I swore the dead possum's odor was lingering on me. I was literally out of my mind, irrational, and didn't care. All I could think about was that Sly was the cause of my craziness. Now he was going to feel the effects.

When I ran into Candi, she told me to relax and to go home, but I didn't listen. I stayed in the projects, waiting for Sly, hoping and wishing he would drive down the street. I was so ready to confront him. Threats took me to another level.

"Don't talk about it; be about it"—that was my motto. Someone was going to get hurt, and for sure, it wasn't going to be me.

Candi said, "Screw that nasty ass. He ain't worth it."

I wasn't hearing it. He had threatened me. Yeah, I might be from Jersey, but I was bout' it. Long hair, don't care; with the wig or without. I don't know why people think that suburban females can't fight. I think the fresh air, trees, grass, and politeness confuses some people.

My dad put me in karate class when I was five. I grew up fighting and breaking boards as a hobby. Most girls play with doll babies. Not me. I was running up and down stairs, doing sit ups and flips, and practicing how to get out of holds because I thought it was fun.

I had earned my first-degree black belt. Combine that with being cuckoo for Cocoa Puffs, and that was a combination for dat ass. Whooping someone's behind was like riding a bike for me. I was passionate about fighting in tournaments where winning was a must.

Over the years, my martial arts skills earned me respect in the world of the Korean martial arts Tang Soo Do. I was the only girl that would fight boys and win in the early eighties to the mid-nineties. Masters would give me props.

My hands were considered a deadly weapon, and I always tried to follow the five Tang Soo Do codes: (1) loyalty to country,

(2) obedience to parents, (3) honor friendship, (4) no retreat in battle (my favorite), (5) in fighting, choose with sense and honor. My reason always made sense to me.

My dad taught me to respect all and fear none. Fear was scared of me.

My dad taught me not to give two farts about what people say about me, but to just grin and bear it. I would grin and fight; I wasn't bearing nothing.

Sly was used to those so-called wannabe hood chicks. I call them Chihuahuas because all they do is bark in an annoying, high-pitched voice. Shut up already!

I was kooky as I stayed in the Web for about three hours, waiting for Sly. I looked all over for him. I went to his favorite bar. We called it the "Bumpy Road" bar. He wasn't there. He was nowhere to be found. I decided to drive home.

I pulled up to my place to find that my front door had been busted wide open. I knew Sly had done it. My neighbors told me that they saw a tall black man with a shaved head kick the door in, and they called 911. They said when he realized they were watching, he ran back to his car and drove off, but they were able to get his license plate number.

I let them know he was my ex and told them he had gone mad. Thank God, Sly didn't have the chance to vandalize my home. My neighbors were so concerned they said they knew of a shelter for abused women and that they could hide me and my son.

They kept saying, "You and your child's safety is paramount."

They were terrified, but I wasn't. I was thinking about who was going to fix my damn door. This was the milk and cookies', being that my door didn't come off the hinges, my handy man was able to temporarily fix it that evening.

But I was still hot grits mad. I called Sly, and he answered.

"Until death do us part, and I'm not going to be the one who dies first," I said and hung up.

See, Sly was scared of the cops, being that he already had a criminal record. He knew that he would go back to jail for breaking and entering and that he would get more time for doing it during the day. You know all those yeggs know the law better than the law-abiding citizens. So with that being said, I knew he wasn't coming back to Jersey.

I knew he was shook because the punk kicked my door in while I wasn't home, and he knew I wasn't home. There are no secrets in the projects. The streets are always watching and telling.

Sly is what I call BAN, which stands for bitch-ass nihility—a waste to society. He called back talking shit, but talk is all he did. I interrupted him with a "whatever," told him I'd see him tomorrow, and hung up.

He called back and said in his BAN voice, "If you come over here and try to do something to me, I'm going to go away, away, away. I mean all the way away to protect myself."

"Coot, stop stuttering and go find your life," I said before hanging up on him again.

I couldn't sleep all night. I tossed and I turned. I got up and paced the floor thinking of a plan to finally get this dude.

Around six the next morning, I drove to Sly's apartment. A young boy who used to live there had shown me how to get in the door without a key. He was always losing his key. I was pleased to discover it still worked.

I quietly ran up the stairs and put a bunch of thumb tacks on the floor in front of his door. Yes, his door had been replaced already. Then I went back outside to get one of the crackhead hookers.

"You want to make some money?" I asked her.

She hesitated, looked around and scratched her head. It was an awkward moment of silence. I think she thought I wanted her so I gave her the gas face.

"Sweetie, I'm strictly dickly."

"What do you want me to do?" she asked.

I told her to knock on Sly's door and pretend like she wanted to cop some drugs. I gave her $20, and we went upstairs. I stood to the side of the door.

Sly must have looked through the peep hole.

"What do you want," he shouted from behind the closed door.

"Some rock," she shouted back.

"Wait a minute."

Quietly I warned her to move back because of the tacks. Sly opened the door, and just as I expected, he stepped out in his bare feet. After he fell to ground, the crackhead grabbed the drugs and ran. Then I stabbed Sly with an ice pick.

Blood was everywhere, and I promise you I saw his jejunum, and that's what snapped me back to reality.

I ran down the stairs and to the car. While I drove back to Jersey, I thought I had just killed my baby dad.

Oh my god, I thought. *What if I really killed him? I made a bad mistake. Oh my god, what am I going to do?*

The possibility that I killed him hit me hard. By the time I reached Kay's house, I was hysterical.

"That bitch ass deserved to die," she told me. "Stop trippin', Twinkle. Sly put you through too much hell, and hell is where he belongs."

"I'm pregnant with his baby, Kay. We've been together off and on for six years. What did I do? I wasn't thinking, and I'm so sorry."

I wanted the opportunity to tell Sly I was sorry and to explain that the hurt and pain he had caused me was just too much.

What am I going to do? I wondered, when the news started reporting, "Black man found stabbed to death. If anyone has information that might lead to the arrest of the suspect, call..." and a hot line number shows up at the bottom of the TV screen.

What if Sly's family offers award money and the crackhead reports me? She can identify me. Everybody in the Web can identify me. They knew I was looking for Sly and that I was mad.

I'm pregnant, and I'm going to be in jail for the rest of my life. I'm going to have my baby in jail. Li'l Man is going to live without a mom. My new baby is going to live without a mom. I was shook.

I went home and called Sly from a blocked number, hoping he would pick up the phone, but he didn't. My heart was beating so fast. So many things were going through my mind. I worried to the point that I started vomiting. I couldn't stop shaking. I just wanted him to pick up his damn phone so I could hear his voice; then I would hang up.

Two weeks passed, and I still didn't know if Sly was alive or not. Sly never picked up his phone. I watched the news for two weeks straight *noint* and still didn't know if Sly was alive. However, nothing was reported on the news.

Three weeks after the incident, Candi called me. "Twinkle, Sly is going around telling people that you crazy and that you stabbed him."

"What? Sly is alive?"

"Yes, girl, and he strutted in the bar shitty sharp. And he's been in the bar telling people that you pregnant too."

Chapter 7
Surprise

I was relieved Sly wasn't dead. I didn't tell many people that I was pregnant because I was contemplating an abortion. I told Diamond that I was thinking about an abortion, and she told me that although Sly ain't shit, she wasn't feeling an abortion this time. My sis was always trying to analyze a situation.

Diamond believes I need a daughter to calm me down and to bring out my sensitive side. I was tough with Li'l Man because I didn't want him to grow up to be a sissy.

My handsome, smart, gifted, and quiet son was all about fun around me, but with others, he would sit back and observe. He knew and saw too much. He loved and cared for me and was overprotective sometimes.

I raised him similar to the way my father raised me. I taught him to respect all and fear none. My son wasn't fearful of anything or anybody. Kids picked on him because he was small and quiet. Those kids had a rude awakening.

He was also a black belt in karate. He was strong, his anger was controlled by reason, and he was very competitive. Losing was something we didn't do. Still I taught my son that our losses are gains.

I love my son so much, and through everything, he was the one that was always there for me. He would tell me he loved me, and when he would see me cry, he would ask, "Mommy, why are you crying?" He wiped my tears away with his little hands. I would tell him I was crying because I had a bad headache. Then I would kiss his forehead and smile at him. My son gave me hope.

One day, Li'l Man and I were just chilling around the house, and I noticed a big smile on his face.

"Boy, what you smiling for?"

"I think God answered my prayers."

I asked "He did?"

"He did. Yes, Mommy."

"How did God do that?"

"When I was five," he explained, "I asked, 'God could I have a big birthday party when I turned six?' And you gave it to me. On that day, I made another wish."

Interrupting him, I said, "Li'l Man, don't tell me your wish because it won't come true."

"But it already came true, Mommy."

"Well, since it already came true, I guess you can tell me."

"You're pregnant," a broad smile lit up his face.

"Li'l Man, who told you that?"

He explained that he made the wish during his birthday party. I had told him then that he couldn't tell me his wish, but I failed to be clear that he couldn't tell anyone, so he told Aunt Diamond.

"I told her that I asked God for a baby sister," he said. "And that's when she told me that you were pregnant."

"Li'l Man, why did you wish for a baby sister?"

He answered, "Because I'm bored on the weekends because we don't have cable. And I don't want to share my toys with a brother. I want to protect my sister the way I protect you."

"Oh! That's the reason why, you enjoy going over Aunt Diamond's house so much because she has cable. Little boy, you are too smart."

I hugged him and said, "Being that you prayed to God for a sister, I believe he will answer your prayer. And as soon as I get some extra money, I promise we'll get cable so you can watch all your cartoons."

I was around twelve weeks pregnant at the time, so an abortion was out of question.

I was pregnant with Sly's baby before and intended to have an abortion. When the ultrasound tech checked the baby's heart prior to the abortion procedure, she had a look of concern on her face.

"Sweety, are you sure that you are pregnant?" she asked.

"I wouldn't be here if I wasn't," I told her.

The baby had died before I could abort it. I did experience some bleeding and cramping beforehand, but I didn't pay it that much attention. The doctors went ahead with the abortion procedure. This would ensure the baby was completely removed so that I wouldn't be exposed to any kind of poison from having a dead baby inside of me.

Yes, Mercedes and I were pregnant at the same time, and

we both lost our babies. I only told Diamond that I was pregnant. That's why she said she wasn't feeling an abortion this time. Diamond believed the last pregnancy must not have been in God's will.

Diamond's insight was always on point. I don't care how much weed and wet she smoked; she loved the Lord. I trusted my sister's intuition because I knew she loved me.

She always had my back although we didn't hang much. She had her own set of friends, but I knew she was just one phone call away, and I was fine with that.

See, in life, too many people want you to be at their beck and call. When you can't be there for some reason, they get emotionally disturbed and want to curse you out. All the times you were there for them before doesn't matter.

Those people have control issues and you need not to be bothered with them. If you stay around them, you will begin to feel anxious, like you're walking on egg shells. This is another form of an ungodly soul tie whether it's a friendship, relationship, or family. Don't allow people to hold you spiritually hostage or keep you in bondage by any means necessary. Your life is much more valuable.

Sometimes your friend or relative won't be there for you. That doesn't make them a bad person. It's possible that God is trying to get you to depend solely on him. This is real rap.

In life, people grow up and grow apart. Reason being some people don't want to grow up or some people don't want you to grow up. I consider those types of people to have a dependency issue. Either which way, get over it and keep it moving. Don't let it be your issue.

It's unfortunate but some people just don't want to see you get ahead, and, just like crabs in a barrel, they will try to pull you back down to where they are. Nah, that ain't cool. Don't allow anyone to pull you down. Stay coming up like throw up. Word!

I continually called Sly and left messages telling him that I was sorry. He didn't respond. The rejection felt worse than if he had cussed me out. At least if he was cursing me out, I would know that he still cared.

Through it all, I learned that rejection is often God's way of redirecting you to a new and better direction. But while I was going through it, I didn't care.

I called Candi to ask if she had seen Sly.

"Yeah, girl. He's messing with that girl Talaya that lives in the back of the projects. She kind of favors you. For a minute, when I first saw them together, I thought it was you. Child, I had to do a double take."

I didn't recognize the name, so I asked who this Talaya was. Candi described her as just a bit browner than me and said her butt is bigger than mine. I still didn't recognize her, but it didn't matter to me. Sly was messing with someone that looked like me. This could only mean that he misses me.

Candi continued saying that the girl has two kids—a boy and a girl. Her mom just died and left her a house on Sulberry

Street. Sly is moving in with her.

Candi told me all that I needed to know. I told you the hood always had the official tapes.

The way I saw it, I had to prove a point. I was going to be Sly's baby mom, and Sly belongs to me.

Sly ain't moving in with nobody, please! And who in the hell is Talaya? I said to myself.

A road trip to Philly was in my near future. I had to investigate. It didn't matter that I was on sick leave because my pregnancy was now considered to be high risk after I fell down a few steps at work because someone spilled some water.

My soul was tied to Sly, and I had the product of our love growing inside of me. I wasn't going to let him go that easily. Nah, it wasn't going down like that, not on my watch.

The next day, when Li'l Man got home, he ate left over spaghetti, and Aunt Diamond came to pick him up and take him back to her place for the night. I gave him a hug and a kiss and told him to have fun.

I thanked my sister for helping me out. She didn't mind watching Li'l Man because he was a thinker and didn't bother her. She loved being around smart people; maybe that's why she studied psychology.

After they left, I got my six-month pregnant self-dolled up. I put on a cute shirt and some tights and slid my swollen feet into some stilettos. On a scale of one to ten, my oomph was a thousand.

I didn't need to tell Candi I was on my way. As long as she

had something to drink, she was good.

What am I going to do when I see Sly? I wondered.

Whatever is going to happen is going to happen, I decided.

When I hit the block, everyone was outside and someone's system was jamming to Notorious B.I.G. "One More Chance."

Someone hollered, "Jersey! What's good?"

People seemed happy to see me, and I felt the love.

Someone else asked, "Who dat?" He was referring to my obvious pregnancy.

By then, I had taken a seat on one of the two chairs on Candi's porch. I responded, "You already know."

I heard someone say, "Oh shit! The boy Sly finally got you knocked up. Damn!"

Then this guy named Noodles, Sly's cousin, yelled, "Twinkle, I heard you tried to kill him."

"You heard right."

"Yo! Jersey girls are rich, crazy, and fine as hell," Noodles said. "I think it's the fresh air that makes y'all crazy."

I asked him what the fresh air has to do with anything.

He replied, "It makes y'all smart because there isn't no pollution, but y'all are crazy. You fool people because y'all talk proper. The project air is polluted, and what you see is what you get. You already know we crazy. But Jersey is on some different shit. Y'all are like chameleons. Wherever you go, you fit in. Y'all get away with murder because your rich parents can afford lawyers for y'all crazy asses."

"Noodles, you are off," I said, while laughing.

"Yep," he said with confidence. "That's why they call me Noodles. I know I don't have it all. All my Noodles is gone. I'm 'bout to change my nickname from Noodles to Bananas."

Everybody who was listening was laughing.

Noodles walked over to the porch. Departing from his comedic self, he told me he thought Sly was lying about me being pregnant because I had not been through the hood.

"Well, I'm back," I assured. "And somebody needs to tell him I'm out here."

"Jersey, you crazy."

"Yep! Don't let the proper grammar and the stilettos fool you."

Noodles hugged me before he left. I knew he was going to tell Sly that I was there because the 'hood do what the' hood do.

I went inside. I was right on time for dinner. Candi made Oodles of Noodles and hot dogs.

"Are you serious?" I asked her.

"You damn right, I'm not Sly. If you don't want to eat it this, then walk your pregnant ass to the Chinese store."

She walked away mumbling something about countless hours smoking blunts on her porch and that I should have brought food.

"Pour yourself something to drink and shut the hell up," I yelled after her. "That's what I'm talking about, just barking."

She turned back and said, "Twinkle, I know your pregnant and all, but I will still cuss your pregnant ass clean out."

I walked outside while shaking my head with my bowl of Oodles of Noodles and hot dogs.

I saw Sly pulling up, and I sat there. I knew he was going to come over to the porch for the simple fact that he hadn't seen me in four months. One of two things was going to happen. Either he was going to cuss me out or he was going to be nice.

Don't you know he tried to act like he wasn't coming? I stared at him. He stared back. I licked my lips slowly, seductively. He knew what that meant and nodded. We both knew we were cool.

I thought, *I got him. By the time I count to twenty, he'll be over here.*

He was there when I reached sixteen.

"What's up, baby mom?"

"You, baby dad."

I stood and gave him a hug. As I held him, I apologized again for stabbing him.

He said there was no need for an apology. "VP, I'm sorry for putting you through that. I deserved what I got. Afterward, I couldn't face you. I decided to leave you alone because I was tired of putting you through that, especially now since you have my seed inside of you."

He paused and looked at me.

"Look at you, girl. Your face got fat, and I ain't even going to say anything about that stomach of yours. But you still sexy. Every time I see you, my knees buckle and I start feeling nervous like I got the butterflies or something. Baby, I miss you. I miss your scent. I miss your smart-ass mouth. I miss my family."

"Can your love rescue me tonight?" I asked him.

"Did you find out what you are having," he asked.

I told him no with an attitude because he totally ignored my question.

"I heard that you're messing with a girl named Talaya."

"Twinkle, we haven't been together in four months."

"Okay. What does that mean?"

"VP, I have needs," he responded.

"And I don't."

"Twinkle, let's cut right through the chase. What is it that you want?"

I answered his question with two questions. "What do you think? Are you coming over tonight?"

"Yeah," he replied.

"I thought so."

Then Candi chimed in, "Oh boy, here we go with the back and forth okeydoke. I'm sick of the both of y'all."

I rolled my eyes and told Candi, "Go ahead somewhere and eat your overcooked Oodles of Noodles."

"They weren't overcooked when you were eating them shits." She was more like a big sister, but she was garrulous. However, she was there for me in her hood-drunken way. She had a heart of gold.

Sly told me to go home, and he would be there shortly. "I got to make some more money. I will be there. I promise."

I knew Sly would come because when he said he promised, he was serious. But I still was feeling some type of way because, in past, we would drive off together.

Chapter 8
Open

I got home and straightened up my messy place. Around ten o'clock, the doorbell rang.

"Are you hungry?" he asked.

I said, "Hungry for you."

"Let's take a bubble bath together. I want to relax."

"Babe, I don't know if we are both going to be able to fit now," I said, rubbing my stomach.

"VP, we will fit," he insisted.

"Okay," I said. But if our two big asses get stuck, all I'm going to say is 'I told you so."

I started the water and lit scented candles. When the bath was ready, we undressed each other.

"Damn, baby mom, look at your stomach," he said and started kissing my belly.

Just then the baby kicked.

"Oh shoot! Our baby is a fighter just like you," he said.

We laughed.

Sly got in the tub first. I got in front of him and laid back on his chest. We talked until the water got cold and the bubbles were gone. Our fingers had that raisin look—you know how they look when you've been in the water too long. Then we took a quick shower because you know after sitting in the tub for a long time you still need to shower.

We dried each other off and went into the bedroom where we started kissing. He started kissing my sensitive spots, and then moved down until his tongue was in my secret place.

I grabbed his bald head with both hands and moved my hips to the rhythm of his tongue. Slowly, he returned to my ear and whispered, "Get your battery-operated toy."

"Why," I asked.

"Because I don't want to hurt you or the baby."

This would be our first time making love in a long time, and I was ready.

"You are not going to hurt me," I muttered.

"Will you just go with the flow, mouth almighty," he said. I gave him the whatever look.

I got the toy. He gently put it in and moved it back and forth slowly while he touched himself. Watching him please himself was such a turn on. It made me want him inside me even more.

"Sly, I want to feel you now," I moaned.

He went in and teased me with the tip for about twenty minutes until he had me where he wanted me to be, and we exploded together.

Sly cried while holding me and promised that he would never hurt me again and said he doesn't wanna be a player no more. I said to myself *Okay, Joe.* He said before he did, he would remember how his feet felt when he stepped on the thumb tacks and how that ice pick felt in his side.

"VP, how did you kill the possum," he asked.

I told him I shot it.

"Babe, when that thing fell out the mink, I screamed like a bi-atch!"

We chuckled and then went to sleep.

The good book says, "There is a way that seems right to man, but in the end it leads to death."

I believed Sly was serious this time. His kisses felt genuine. I felt the connection again. This time it was real.

The next morning, Diamond dropped off Li'l Man before school. Sly got him ready for school, fixed him breakfast, and walked him to the bus stop.

I woke up to scrambled eggs, toast, turkey bacon, and blueberry muffins. We had breakfast in bed. My honey was back, and I was satisfied.

We laid around for most of the morning, and he caught me up with the hood tapes.

I asked him, "What's up with that girl?"

He said, "You're my wife, and you don't have to worry 'cause I'm here with you."

I told Sly, to handle the situation ASAP because "Twinkle got what you want and what you need."

Sly responded, "Twinkle, you are not Nicole Ray or Missy."

"But I do make it hot, and you know this."

There was no competition because you see where Sly was at. I just wanted to put that out there. When it came to Sly, I was cocky. I knew none of his other women could compete with what we had, our longevity, and our sexual compatibilities.

Sly confirmed that. He said we fit like a glove.

"I won't let no chick ever disrespect you. I will break a brick and make medicine sick when it comes to my vanilla pound cake. Everybody knows it," he paused. The hood knows that you got me."

"I know and I ain't beat. When Jersey pulls up, I get much respect. I can walk and do anything there because I am Sly's girl. I am that chick. I am the girl Twinkle, and none of those hoes can walk a mile in my shoes."

Sly and I did good for about two months. Then one Wednesday, Sly called me early and asked if I could pick him up. He said he didn't feel like hustling today. His car was acting up so he just wanted to chill.

I asked what was wrong with his car.

He said it kept cutting off while he was driving, so he took it to the shop.

So I picked him up, and we came back to Jersey. Sly did his usual cooking and cleaning. While he cleaned the bathroom, I watched *Jerry Springer*. I was in my bag. Then my phone rang. It was Candi.

"Oh shit!"

I knew Candi was calling me with some tapes about Sly,

and I knew it wasn't good because she never calls me unless it is something major.

I answered the phone, "Hey, girl! What's going on?"

In her loud, raspy voice, she asked if I had seen Sly.

"Yeah, he's here cleaning the bathroom."

She replied, "That is where he needs to be because he is full of shit."

"What happened?" I asked.

She said, "Talaya set his car on fire, and it blew clean up."

"When did this happen?"

"Last night. Child, someone told Sly they saw her putting gasoline on his car, and Sly went over her house and whooped her ass bad."

"Why would Talaya do that?"

"Because Sly was with his other woman the day before," Candi told me. "He was riding her in his car on the avenue, and Talaya saw them. Talaya approached Sly and was like you messing with me, Twinkle, and this other girl. See, Sly never stopped messing with Talaya. She asked him for her house key back. Sly told her that he wasn't giving her shit and told her to get out of his face. Sly told the chick in the car he didn't even know who Talaya was. Come to find out, the chick in the car is from North Philly. Val was standing outside ear-hustling and recognized her from the salon. She was telling people that she's been messing with Sly for about eight months. Girl, you won't even believe who she is."

"Who is she?"

"The girl Buf."

"Buf?"

"Yeah," Candi said. "You remember her from the projects. She moved to Richard Allen."

"No," I answered.

Candi said, "Yes, you do, Twinkle. Bonita, but we call her Buf for bootie hall of fame. Remember her now? She has five guys' names tattooed on each ass cheek. Sly is number ten because she like the way he be hitting it from the back. What I hear is that she knows all about you, but Sly gave her and his other women eight rules they had to follow."

"What?" I said in disbelief. "What are the rules?"

Candi said hold up. She had to get the paper.

"I had to write this shit down." She read, "Rule one: when you see the red car with Jersey tags, that is my baby mom. Rule two: if you are walking or driving and see my baby mom, go the total opposite direction. Rule three: walk or drive to the nearest corner and fall back to see if I (Sly) get into his vehicle or hers. Rule four: if I do get in the car or her car, that means I'm going to Jersey, but I will be back. Rule five: don't call me. Rule six: I repeat don't call me. I will call you when I come back to Philly because I don't want no trouble with my baby mom while I'm in Jersey because you know she is crazy, and I don't want no dead rodents at my door. Rule seven: baby, never get mad because I will be back. I promise. Rule eight: remember that I care for you and my baby mom and I don't want either one of you to feel disrespected."

"Candi, this is unbelievable. How did you get the rules?"

She said Val is good friends with Buf's cousin who told Val that rule eight is Buf's favorite and that their favorite song is "Seven Days" by Mary J.

I replied, "Oh, that's why she's snappin' because it's Wednesday and he went away. And on Thursday she knows things aren't going to be the same. Ain't that some shit?"

"Sly is just nasty along with his gutter rats," Candi said. "I wish a dude would give me some dumb rules to follow. I would tell him to follow this big ass and to get the hell out of here."

"I know that's right, Candi. Good looking out." The water in the bathroom stopped, so I told her I'd call her back.

Sly walked in the bedroom, kissed my forehead, and sat on the bed.

My leg was shaking because I am like, *Here we go again.*

"Why are you looking like that," he asked?

I said, "Looking like what?"

"Mad," Sly said.

"What happened to your car," I asked again.

"I'm not sure, VP. I tried to start it, and for some reason it wouldn't start," Sly said with a straight face.

"Sly, I'm going to ask you one more time. What happened to your car?"

"Babe, why are you trippin' about my car? Let's get dressed and drive to the park."

I thought, *This dude knows how to lie too damn good.* All that cooking, cleaning, and loving was nothing but compensation because he knew all along what he was doing.

I understood the saying, "The way to a man's heart is through his stomach." That's also the way to a woman's heart. My heart was with Sly. But on this day, I made up my mind never again to go back. I'm done for good. I had endured enough of Sly's games, and I wasn't playing anymore.

He was the master manipulator, womanizer, liar, and officially an addict.

"Sly, who was the girl riding in your Lexus with the tats all over her ass?"

"That was my sister."

"Your sister? When did your sister move to North Philly?"

"What are you talking about?" Sly asked.

I jumped up and out of my bed and pointed my finger clean in his face. "Punk, I'm asking the questions."

So Sly said something about me interrogating him and not owing me an explanation. He then had the nerve to say with a mischievous smile, "Stop trying to intimidate and incriminate me because I'm here with you." Sly said that like he had a capital "S" on his chest. He really thought he said something major just now because he used three "I" vocabulary words sounding like Rev. Jesse Jackson.

"Ooh!" You! Irritating, ingrate, indolent, idiot! I snapped. "You ain't the only one that knows "I" vocabulary words. And you are not doing me a favor because your black ass is here? As a matter of fact, I'm doing your dumb ass a favor. And I'm going to do you one better and take your ass to the bus stop so you can get right on the 409 bus."

"Take me the hell home," he ordered.

"Okay." We got in my car, and I drove his ass right to the bus stop.

He started yelling saying that he should punch me in my face. I dared him to and told him that would be reason to bury his ass in these woods.

"Do it, Sly. You king ding-a-ling? Do it! Go ahead!"

He snatched my keys out of the ignition and ran out of the car. When I got out to chase him, he got in the car and drove off.

I'm eight months pregnant, and I'm standing at the bus stop looking like nobody knows the trouble I've seen and nobody knows my sorrows. I have no car, no keys to the car or my house. This dude has all of my keys and my car. It is mid-July, and it is hot. I started walking. A sweet Caucasian lady saw me and asked if I was okay.

I told her what had happened, and she took me to the police station. I was thankful for the ride. I was wearing sweats and a white T-shirt. My hair was a mess. I was funky and pissed off. I requested to speak to a police officer and explained to him what happened. I told the police to call the Betsy Ross Bridge so they can shut it down. But he just laughed at me.

I asked the officer, "What is so funny?"

"How do you know he is taking the Betsy Ross and not the Tacony Bridge?"

"Because I know! Just do it!"

"Ma'am I can't do that."

"I will handle this on my own!" I yelled and stormed out the room.

I called Kay. She agreed to pick me up and drive me to Philly. My car was parked in front of Candi's house. Candi wasn't home, so I knocked on Candi's neighbor's door, Ms. Bonnie. She was an older neighbor, and she was cool. She knew Sly and his family well. In fact, she used to babysit Sly.

She hadn't seen Sly and asked me what happened. So I told her the story.

"Twinkle, stop acting so stupid. You have good sense. You are better off without him."

"Yes, ma'am," I sighed.

I gave her Kay's number and asked that if she saw Sly if she would ask him for my keys and call me at Kay's.

Kay drove me around to look for that dummy for about an hour and a half. He was nowhere to be found. We stopped by his apartment. If he was home, he didn't answer his door. Sly was good at hiding. He was such a little boy.

When we got back to Kay's house, there was a message from Ms. Bonnie. She had my keys.

I called her back and told her that we would be there within twenty minutes.

"Take your time," she said. "I'm not going anywhere."

When we arrived, Ms. Bonnie gave me the keys. I thanked her.

"Twinkle, leave Sly alone. He brings out the worst in you. Do you even know what your best is?" Then Ms. Bonnie continued to say Twinkle you need to be with someone who brings the best out of you and not the stress in you.

All I could do was give her a look of sorrow.

Truth is, I didn't know what my best was. I felt like I was too deep in this relationship. As much as I wanted to leave Sly alone, I always went back to him for some crazy reason.

Why should I leave him? At least I know what I'm dealing with. I know all his chicks, all his game, and I am Sly's number one woman. Everybody knew about me. What do I have to lose? I'm still that girl Twinkle, numero uno, to death do us. I'm pregnant, and for real, where am I going? Besides, all dudes are players. They are all the same. They just wear different jeans.

While Kay and I were driving back, Mary J. song "Not Gon' Cry" was playing on the car's radio. I was so depressed. I couldn't see no way out of this relationship with Sly. I tried to cry, but I was so angry that I couldn't.

So many things were going through my mind. I was about to have his baby in one month. He ain't shit. Now I'm going to have two dumb-ass baby daddies who are not going to be involved in their child's life.

All the years invested with Sly were a waste.

I just couldn't believe that I was going to have two baby dads and was not going to be with either of them.

I was ashamed and disgusted.

My kids deserve so much better than this.

Chapter 9
My Heart

A few days later, Grandma had a heart attack and was rushed to the hospital. My mom called to tell me and offered me a ride, but I couldn't wait.

When I arrived, the front desk receptionist told me what room Grandma was in. I ran down the hall.

Grandma was in and out of consciousness. When she was cognitive, she kept saying over and over again, "Pretty girl, God is good."

I got angry. What kind of God would allow her to have a heart attack? What kind of God would do that? What kind of God would allow her to get hurt? Anger blinded me to the blessing that she was still alive and was able to speak.

I remembered Grandma preach about God's ways not being our ways and his thoughts not being our thoughts, but I was still angry that she was in the hospital from a heart attack. At that time, I didn't want to hear anything about God. I felt like God and I were not in good standings.

Every day I would go to the hospital. It appeared that Grandma was getting better. She would always tell me not to give up on God. I would tell my Grandma that God gave up on me a long time ago.

"Baby, that is a trick of the enemy," she warned me. "God

is good, and he loves you. Satan is the father of all lies, and he is the author of confusion."

In my head, I heard *Blah, blah, blah.*

"Grandma, you need to live so you can see your great-grandbaby," I pleaded.

She smiled and said, "I'm praying for Li'l Man and the other miracle that you are carrying."

"Grandma, don't worry about me. Just worry about yourself and get better."

"I'm believing in God for you to return back to Christ," she responded. "Seek ye first the kingdom of God and all his righteousness and all these things shall be added unto you."

I loved Grandma more than anyone on this earth besides Li'l Man, Diamond, and my parents. She and I had a special bond. Grandma always had a way of making me feel like everything was going to be alright.

Despite my earlier anger, I prayed that God would heal Grandma completely and started humming "Precious Lord" by Mahalia Jackson while tears were rolling down my face. I begged God not to take her away. I believed that God was going to heal her because I had faith and so did she. Grandma started getting better, and the doctors told the family that she should be coming home in a few more days if all of her blood work comes back good.

God was healing Grandma. I started to believe in God again. I remembered Grandma telling me that once you believe in

God, you must believe that there is an adversary.

The devil is real too.

She used to say, "Pretty girl, demons are smarter than some humans because even the demons believe in God and tremble."

She then went to say it's a sad shame that some people lack reverence for God. She said, "Pretty girl, we are living in perilous times."

I thought that was so deep.

My baby was due in one month. In one more month, Grandma would bless my baby. The thought of that made me smile.

A few days later, Diamond called me around nine in the morning to see if she could come over. That was fine with me, but I reminded her that I was leaving around 12:30 p.m. to visit Grandma. She insisted that we ride together.

She rang the doorbell around 9:15 a.m.

"Dang, that was fast," I said as I opened the door.

Diamond was standing there with a troubled look on her face.

"Who did what? I got bail money so let's do what we got to do. Just give me a few minutes to get my heat."

"Nah, sis, we don't have to kill nobody today."

"Okay, well what's good," I asked.

She said, "Sis…"

"Why are you acting like this? You know how that pisses

me off when people beat around that stupid bush."

Diamond responded, "I know, sis."

"So what's wrong," I asked.

"Grandma passed earlier this morning," she began to cry.

"No, Grandma didn't die. She is getting better."

She said, as she wiped her tears. "Sis, Grandma is gone."

I sat down and started bawling. I cried and cried and cried some more.

Li'l Man hugged me and said, "Mommy, Grandma is sleeping on earth but is awake in heaven."

"Yes, she is, baby," I said to him. But inside I was screaming "God! How could you?"

Why did God take her away from me? She was my strength, my joy, and my love.

What kind of God are you?

Diamond drove us all to the hospital. She was worried about me going into premature labor.

At the hospital, we ran into Ms. Bonnie. She was visiting her cousin who just had a stroke. Ms. Bonnie knew Grandma well. She visited the church down through the years. I told her about Grandma. She gave her condolences and I thanked her.

"Make sure you keep me posted on when Mother Munford's funeral is," she said.

My parents, cousins, aunts, and uncles were already in Grandma's room. Diamond, Li'l Man, and I brought the number to about forty. The older generation was praying while the younger ones were crying.

Grandma was the rock to all of us. We stayed there for a couple hours reminiscing on the positive affect she had on us.

Afterward, my sister took me and Li'l Man home. All I wanted to do was sleep, but my sister stayed for a little while, and we talked. She appeared to feel a little better after she smoked her blunt, but that was only temporary. When she left, I tucked Li'l Man in and sat on my couch and cried until my eyes were swollen and I didn't have any more tears. I remembered Grandma telling me that God understands the language of our tears because sometimes you just can't articulate the hurt you are feeling. However, I did articulate this prayer because I needed to be specific. I wanted God to hear and answer.

"God, you took my Grandma from me and she loved you. God, I know I'm a backslider, but I remember Grandma telling me that you are married to the backsliding. Meaning, you still love me and that you are still concerned about my well-being because your love is not conditional. Yes, I'm pregnant. Yes, I'm not married, but one thing I do know is that you are married to me. Because I know that you still love me regardless of all of my nasty sins, I pray that this baby that I'm carrying be a healthy girl. Please, Father, let this baby give me the joy and the love that my grandma used to give me. Please and let this baby be a reminder to me that Grandma is still here, just in a different form. In Jesus's name, amen."

Now don't get me wrong, Li'l Man was always there for

me, but, in my eyes, a girl would represent my grandma.

When I woke up the next morning, I felt like I was dying inside. I told myself that I must live for my son and for my baby. I really didn't care about myself, but I do love and care about my kids. Sometimes your kids will be your only strength when all hope is gone.

I thought, *What if God answers my prayer and blesses me with a little girl?*

I kept saying to myself that I will live and not die and that I will not lose my mind because Grandma is not here. Besides, Grandma wouldn't want to look down from heaven to see me in a crazy hospital.

I could hear her saying, "Pretty girl, get your mind right and turn to Jesus."

When Li'l Man woke up, I asked if he wanted breakfast.

"No, Mommy, I'm going to make you breakfast."

Mind you Li'l Man is six. He just wanted his mommy to feel better.

He walked his little self into the kitchen, climbed on the kitchen counter, and grabbed a box of cereal that was on top of the refrigerator. He put some whipped cream on top of the frosted flakes and brought me the bowl.

"Eat, Mommy," he told me.

I smiled and cried.

"Mommy, you have to eat because my brother or sister is hungry."

I was still crying, so he started to feed me.

"Everything will be okay. Isn't that what you tell me? God will make everything better. He did it for me because we have cable now, and I'm about to have a baby brother or sister."

Li'l Man was serious about that cable. Aunt Diamond turned him on to the cartoon network and that was all she wrote.

I smiled. "I love you so much. Give me a huggy and a kissy," as I sniffled.

I continued eating my breakfast.

"This is the best cereal I have ever had," I said. "What made you put whipped cream on top of the cereal?"

"Sly, would fix my cereal this way."

"Oh really."

"Yeah, Mommy. He told me not to tell you because you didn't need to know. He said it is between the brothers, and he would give me a pound."

"Do you and Sly have any more secrets?" I asked.

"Mommy, promise you're not going to get mad," he responded.

"Of course not. What is it?" I said anxiously.

"When you used to be sleep, we would talk and he taught me how to play chess. Sly taught me how to outsmart my opponent."

"*Opponent*," I said. "That's a big word. What do you know about an opponent?"

"An opponent is someone who competes against me."

My Li'l Man Shaquan was growing up before my eyes.

"Sly also gave me something and told me not to tell you. I told Sly that I hoped that you would always keep the cable on, so he gave me $300. He said if the cable ever gets cut off, I should give the money to you so you can turn it back on."

"Shaquan, let me find out you have a stash."

"I do, Mommy," he bragged.

Then I asked, "Do you and Sly have any more secrets?"

"Yeah."

"What else?" I asked.

"Sly would always tell me to take care of you because I'm the man of the house when he is not here. He would tell me to be a better man than him when I grow up because I have a good mom. He told me to listen to you and to my teachers so I could have a good job. And he told me not to take no shit from nobody because this is a dog-eat-dog world. Sly told me that life is like chess, and I should always know about my opponent."

"Shaquan, just because this is Mommy's first time calling you by your government name, it does not mean you are grown and can say cuss words." I didn't address what he had shared about Sly.

"I know, Mommy. I'm sorry, but I was just telling you what Sly told me."

"Well, you got that off today, and you just used your no-butt-whoopin' card. Next time, Mommy is not going to be so nice," I said, but inside I was cracking up. He made me feel so much better.

I asked Shaquan if he knew where the money was. He said yes. Sly helped him clean his closet and told him to keep it clean so he could always find the money.

"I'll show you, Mommy," he said as he started to walk toward his room.

I followed Shaquan to his room. His closet looked like a little man's department store. It was so neat. All his clothes were hung up. Shaquan was always neat, but I never knew Sly had helped him clean his closet. Obviously, there were a lot of things I didn't know probably because majority of the time, I would be asleep and wouldn't wake up until Sly fixed dinner.

Shaquan stood on his chair and put his little hand inside the pocket of his polo jeans.

"Here it is, Mommy," he said while showing me three crisp hundred-dollar bills.

"Shaquan, Sly taught you how to fold your jeans and hang up your shirts," I asked.

"Yes. He taught me how to lace my sneakers and clean them too. He gave me this stuff called Afta. It's real strong and might burn me, so I had to promise not to use it."

"What exactly does it do?" I asked.

"It takes the skid marks out," he said as if it was hard to believe I didn't know the answer.

"Well, excuse me for not knowing what it does," I said while being sarcastic.

We laughed.

Sly was always cleaner than the board of health, at least on the outside. We went back into the living room. Shaquan sat on my lap while we watched TV. I ordered his favorite Chinese food for dinner. We just chilled all day.

I never again considered him my Li'l Man. He was Shaquan, my son. He was my Big Boy now.

The next day, Sly called to express his deepest sympathy. Ms. Bonnie told him about Grandma. He said he cried a few tears and remembered when he met her. It was a couple of years ago at her house for Christmas dinner. They had a talk, which to this day, I still don't know what about.

Everybody in the Web knew Grandma. Her church was five blocks away, and she did a lot of street ministry.

Sly said sometimes he would see Grandma handing out Christian Tapes, and he would speak to her. She would tell him that she was praying for him and would give him a hug. Sly knew how much I loved her.

"I'm sorry for your loss, and I'm sorry for hurting you again. I don't mean to hurt you, but shit happens."

"Shit happens, Sly! We are about to have a baby, and your name is tattooed on Buf's ass, and you want me to act like nothing happened! Shit happens! Furthermore, you stole my car. What the hell do you want me to do?"

Sly responded, "Let me help you mourn. You have my

baby inside of you, and I just want to be there for you and Li'l Man."

I wanted Sly to hold me so bad. I was vulnerable. I just wanted to cry. Listening to "Emotions" by H-Town didn't make it any better. I wanted to hear him say, "Baby, everything is going to be okay." I just wanted Sly here because I missed his company.

"Do you know anything about the funeral?" he asked.

I told him not yet.

"When you find out, can you at least let me know because I want to go with you. And Ms. Bonnie wants to go too. VP, I know that you will be due soon, and I want to be around for you."

"Sly, if you're going to hurt me again, just do us both a favor and leave me alone."

"Is that what you really want?" he asked.

"Sly, stop with the rhetorical questions. What do you want? Do you want me to tattoo your first and last name on both of my tities 'cause you like nasty chicks?"

"VP, I don't love them hoes."

I replied, "Okay, Snoop. I wish you had Snoop's money. Maybe I could deal with your cheating ass a little bit better."

"VP, those chicks are easy. I only mess with them because I be bored, and it is just something to do. I don't treat them the way I treat you. I don't cook for them and chill with their thousands of kids. Matter of fact, I don't do shit for them. I smash them, and I leave them.

Them hoes don't mean nothing to me. Everybody knows

that I love you and Li'l Man. Those bitches be hatin' on you. They really don't know about you and me, and those hoes wish they were you.

Them chicks be saying that you put some kind of voodoo on me because they can't understand why I love you the way I do."

"Voodoo, Sly. That's what they came up with? Tell them to stop listening to D'Angelo, "Send It On." However, I'm sending you on your merry way. No, this ain't voodoo. But they are no frills, pork hot dogs, and I'm a porter house steak. Clearly the two taste totally different. One costs more and taste so much better. They need to go figure, and so do you," I shouted, and then banged on him.

Sly called back. I didn't pick up the phone, but I did after the fifteenth phone call.

"Baby, I know you're pregnant, and you are real emotional, and I'm trying to be patient."

"Patient, my ass, you just ought to know patience. You been through this how many times? Let's see 1, 2, 3, 4, 5, 6, 7, 8, 9, and 10. Ain't that your favorite number anyway? Oh yeah! That's right! You're number ten on Buf's ass. Man, get out of here." Then I banged on him again.

Sly called from a blocked number. I picked up the phone like an idiot because I didn't think he would block his number.

Before I could say anything, I heard him say, "V.P., I'm sorry and I love you and Li'l Man. Yes, I cheated on you, but one thing you can't deny is the love I have for you and your son."

That messed me up because I knew what he said was true.

"Yeah, Shaquan told me about the cereal secret and the money for the cable. But, Sly, I just don't know. I'm tired of this roller coaster ride. It's literally making me sick.

I'm about to have another baby, and Shaquan and my baby need a mother and father who are in a healthy relationship."

"Baby, I'm here."

"But for how long?"

"A lifetime."

"That's such a sentimental response, Sly, but I'm serious."

He began to ramble about his new Escalade truck and how he wanted to take me and Shaquan shopping.

That was the magic word—*shopping*. I had a quick change of heart. "Babe, when you coming?"

"Tomorrow."

"Why tomorrow?" I asked. "See, this is the shit I'm talking about."

"VP, I have to make some money before I come through if I'm going to take you shopping."

"Whatever," I said and hung up.

He called back. I told him to leave me alone.

"VP, I love you. Let me get this money."

"What does love have to do with anything. Your love hurts." So Sly banged on me.

"No, this punk didn't just hang up on me!" I said as I called him back.

"Baby mom, I'm not going to argue with you. I'm going to see you tomorrow."

Then he hung up on me again. Clearly, I thought, Sly forgot the game. I'm the one who does the hanging up, not him.

I called back, and Sly picked up again and said, "VP, I'm not going to listen to you while you are spraying me with insults. Sly trying to backpedal from the heated argument. I'm calling you on some good shit and you acting all husky."

"Sly, I can call you a million times if I want to. What the hell are you going to do but pick up the phone and act like a little bitch!"

He hung up again, and my doorbell rang.

"Oh shit," I said, thinking he was at my door. It was Diamond. I was like; yeah Sly ain't crazy for real.

I opened the door and told her that I just finished cussing Sly's ass out. She was coming to check on me because she couldn't get me on the phone. She asked me if I was all right. I said yes and asked if she would watch Shaquan while I drive to Philly real fast.

"Yeah. Sis, I got heat in the car. Do you think you need it?"

"Nah, I'm good."

I called Sly. He didn't pick up, and his machine didn't answer either. I assumed he had disconnected it so I couldn't leave a message. Instead of hanging up, I let it ring while I drove.

When I got to his apartment, the phone was still ringing. He was in his apartment listening to the phone ring the whole time. The look in Sly's eyes when he saw me at his door was so movie.

"Baby mom, you are losing it. I can't believe you called and let the phone ring while driving out here."

"And I can't believe that you let the phone ring all this time," I said as I chuckled.

"VP, you are crazy for real."

We started laughing.

"Come here, girl." He hugged me tight. "I miss your crazy ass."

"Baby, I miss you too."

"Look, I'm not doing nothing. I'm making money, that's it, so I can spend it on you and the kids tomorrow."

"Why don't you get a nine to five?" It was more than a suggestion than a question. "I'm about to have your baby, and this is too risky. What happens if someone tries to rob you or kill you or you get raided and do time? What am I going to do? Who's going to take care of me, Shaquan, and the baby? Sly, don't you think of these things?"

"Yeah, but this is what I do."

"Well, isn't time you stopped? You are forty years old and still hustling. When are you going to change?"

"I am changing because I'm falling in love with you. You have been there for me for six years. No female has ever stuck by me."

"Sly, I don't want no other man, I miss you and need you."

"Baby, I'm here. Stop taking things so personal. I told you this before. You are my wife. Look at you. You all fat in the face with my baby inside of you."

Sly rubbed and kissed my belly and told me to go home and relax.

"I'll be home tomorrow morning."

"Honey, I want to see you tonight," I said, pouting.

He said he'd be there. "Just let me make this money."

"Okay," I said, happier. While R. Kelly Featuring Notorious B.I.G. "(You to Be) Be Happy." Played on the radio, I started two steppin'.

We kissed, and he walked me to my car. By the way, his new truck was mean.

When I got home, Diamond asked what happened. "Nothing, we just talked and kissed. He'll be here tomorrow."

"There's always an unexpected detour messing with you," said Diamond.

"What, sis?" I didn't understand where she was coming from.

"I only came to see how you were doing and to tell you that Grandma's funeral is on Thursday at Christ Deliverance in North Philly. I think we should ride together. Mom and Dad have each other, and we have each other."

"For sure," I said.

We touched fists and said, "Wonder twin powers activate." We loved that cartoon when we were young. We laughed.

"You know today is Monday," Diamond said.

Diamond was off work on Mondays. Being that she did a lot of partying on the weekends, Monday was her "me time" day.

"I'll holla, sis. See you Thursday at 9:15 a.m."

"Peace," I said as she gathered her stuff and went out the door.

We had to get ready for the funeral, so I took Shaquan to the store. I bought him a sharp suit and shoes. I got me a cute black dress with some sharp sandals. Yes, I used the cable money. Then, we went to Red Lobster. Shaquan loved some Red Lobster. He was no McDonald's child.

"Mommy," he said while we were eating, "I told you that everything was going to be okay."

"You sure did," I responded.

In my Ice Cube voice, today was a good day.

We got home around 6:30 p.m., and I had missed a call from Diamond.

I dialed her.

"What's good, sis?"

"Change of plans. Dad and Mom said that we all are meeting in Bensalem at Grandma's house at nine a.m. because Uncle Ted rented four limos for the immediate family. So you have to be ready at eight because I was still going to pick you up. Please be on time because you know how you always run late."

"Sis, I'm already pregnant and tired. Now you are telling me to wake up earlier. I can't make you any promises, but I will try my best."

Shaquan was waiting for me to get off the phone. "Mommy I'm tired. I think I got the itis."

"What you know about the itis." I laughed.

"It's when you eat too much and you get sleepy."

"Boy, you are too much, we laughed some more."

I got him ready for bed, read a bed time story, said our prayers, and gave him a kiss.

As I was walking out the room, Shaquan asked, "Mommy, grandma is with God now, isn't she?"

"Yes, baby. She sure is."

I went into the living room to watch some TV. Then the phone rang. It was Ree. She asked how I was doing. I told her that I'm doing better today. I updated her about the funeral arrangements and told her about the clothes I bought for myself and Shaquan.

"You up for some company," she asked.

"Yeah."

"Your girls will be over in a minute."

Ree, C, Kay, and Bertha were all good and high.

"No y'all *ninjas* didn't come over here like that knowing that I can't smoke," I joked.

"You're the one knocked up, not us," Kay said. "Stop hatin'."

They brought me a big card, which said "We love you" and was signed G4L—girls for life—and an ice-cream cake.

We all hugged.

Kay asked if I heard from Sly. I told her he was coming over tomorrow. She turned on my radio and Mad Cobra's "Flex" was playing.

"Oh! This is my jam," I said while doing the butterfly and snappin' my fingers.

Kay interjected, "That's why you pregnant now."

"Whatever," I said with a raised eyebrow.

She said, "I can't stand him, but I'm going to love my niece or nephew."

Ree said, "I hope your baby don't have his frown mark on its face."

Then C chimed in, "Come on, Sly is not that bad."

"That's like saying that I don't have a big ass," Bertha said. "Everybody knows that I got a big ass."

"Y'all are crazy," I said, adding that the ice cream cake looks good. "I'm about to cut a piece." I love cake and was craving ice cream, so the cake was right on time. I ate my cake while they drank Heinekens.

Then Kay asked me why do I love Sly so much?

"I really can't answer you. But what I can tell you is that I think that I'm supposed to love him, and that's why I love him so much."

Ree responded, "That's some real stuff, Twinkle. Because

123

you are supposed to. That's some deep shit. I ain't ever heard of a reason like that."

"That's real, and that's my honey, and he's sweet like that."

"He stinks like that, Twinkle," Kay said. "He ain't shit. I think that you smoked entirely too much weed, and it damaged a lot of your brain cells."

"Kay, when did you get an A in science?" I asked.

"Me and Ree loved science. It was you, C, and Bertha that was truant."

We laughed.

Bertha replied, "Yeah, you right. We was always cutting class and smoking in the bathroom. Then we would walk to the bakery and get a Jamaican beef patty and that Champagne soda."

"Wow! We were wildin'," I said. We all laughed some more.

"It's almost one a.m., and I have a six a.m. hair appointment. Although I would love to stay, I can't." C said.

I was getting a little sleepy too.

So we all gave each other hugs, and they all left. I started to wind down. As I was getting ready to get in the shower, the doorbell rang.

I said to myself, "Which one of those *n-jays* forgot something? It was probably C because she was always oblivious. It might have been Kay wanting to take a piece of cake for later when she got the munchies."

I looked out the peep hole, and to my surprise, it was Sly. I opened the door.

"Hey, honey, you are right on time."

"On time for what?"

I said, "What you think?"

"I think I just saw Kay and them."

"They just left. They brought me this card and an ice cream cake."

Sly then asked, "How are you?"

"Better now since you're here. But I thought that you were coming over tomorrow?"

"It is tomorrow," he responded.

"You are so corny," I told him.

"That is what your mouth is saying." He smacked my behind.

"I said keep smacking my ass, and I'm going to smack your ass back. And you're going to scream like a little girl."

"There goes that smart-ass mouth."

"Yeah, Negro. You love it and you love me."

"I do," he said, and we kissed.

I told him that I was just about to get in the shower, and he asked if I thought we both could fit.

"You really trying to play me," I said laughing. "I'm not that big."

"Yes, you are," he snickered. "But you are all stomach."

"The baby can come any day now," I said.

"I know. That's why I want us to go shopping so I can buy

the baby some stuff like a stroller and things that I'll need to put together."

"Okay, are you going to take a shower with me?"

"Yeah, why not," Sly said yeah.

We showered and stared at each other.

"Lisa Renee Valentine a.k.a. Twinkle, a.k.a. my soon-to-be baby mom, I love you. I know I did you dirty. But, baby, I never meant to hurt you," he apologized. "When I used to see your grandma from time to time after her church would get out, I would stop and talk with her. She would say, 'Baby, when are you going to jump the broom?' I promised her that I would."

"Sly, why did you lie to my grandma," I asked jokingly.

"Bay, all jokes aside. I promised her, and I'm going to marry you."

"When, Sly?"

"I'm not sure, but I'm promising you like I promised your grandma that I am going to. You know that I don't play with spiritual people like that because they spook me out."

I thought to myself, *There's been a lot of private conversations going around. Grandma took that to her grave because she never told me.* I started crying.

Sly held me tight. The water was hitting his back, but some was still spraying on me. I don't know how long we stayed there, but when we got out, I was so cried out that I went right to sleep.

I woke up to pancakes and fruit along with sausage.

Shaquan and Sly were early birds. They already had played a game of chess, and they were darn near dressed.

"VP, get yourself together so we won't have to be out all day," Sly demanded.

He knew I was cranky in the morning. Since I was pregnant, I was worse. Breakfast in bed improved my mood. I ate, showered, and dressed while they waited for me.

Sly would say that I go to bed like an old white lady. Right after Jeopardy went off; he knew that I was going to bed. This wasn't true, but staying up all night was boring especially since I had a comfortable bed. I swear Sly was jealous of my bed.

"You and this damn bed have a relationship," he would say, while being smart.

"Yeah we do," I'd say, "because it's always here to comfort me unlike your wishy washy ass."

Sly would ignore my comment.

After I ate and got dressed, I started to feel crampy. I told Sly, and he asked if I want him to take me to the hospital. I told him no. I wanted to just flow and play the day out.

We climbed into Sly's Escalade, and he shopped for Shaquan first and then the baby. Sly had good taste. He knew what looked good, smelled good, and what tasted good. He was particular in everything—appearance, quality, color, fabric, but never in the price. He bought a stroller, basinet, crib, play pen, and neutral color clothes.

We went to Gaetano's to eat. Those cheese steaks are to

live for! Philly cheese steaks ain't got nothing on them! You know Philly is known for its cheese steaks.

When we got home, Sly started to rearrange my room to fit the baby's needs. He didn't mind rearranging furniture and organizing closets and drawers. That was just him. Everything had to be easy to find and accessible because when Sly couldn't find something, he would get crazy. He would not stop looking for whatever he lost until he found it. I couldn't understand it. It seemed like Sly was never bothered by anything that I did. The only thing that would piss him off was his own insecurities and his guilt.

Sly is his worst enemy. The drugs, women, and lies had a severe toll on his conscience. The longer we were together, the better I understood.

He was looking for someone or something to fill a void – a void he tried to fill with drugs, alcohol, and women. But they were burying him slowly like quick sand.

Being that I was clean for about eight months, I was able to think with a clear head. You know when you're constantly getting high you are really not in touch with reality and you're unable to deal with life's problems in a healthy nature. It's like a constant dream that allows you to escape reality.

"Taste and see that the Lord is good," that's what Grandma used to say.

After Sly was done rearranging the room, he said he was tired and didn't feel like cooking, so he suggested that we go out for dinner. You know that me and Shaquan was down.

We went to Friday's. After I ate, I felt what I thought was a contraction. We went home, and Sly got Shaquan ready for bed. I just wanted to relax, so I took a bath. I know some old folks say that you shouldn't take a bath before you're dilated to a certain point because it can make the labor longer, but that is an old wives' tale. The way I was feeling, I had to bathe. Sly sat on the toilet and asked how I was feeling.

"A little bit better. Tomorrow, my sister is picking me up for the funeral. The immediate family will be getting in the limos at my grandparent's house."

Sly said he would drive us to the house then follow the limos. I thanked him, as he helped me up and out of the tub, while drying me off.

"Look at those two big jugs."

I told him to be quiet. He started gently kissing both of them.

"Baby, you starting," I asked.

He whispered, "Yeah."

We started kissing, and he unzipped his pants.

"Mr. Long is looking for Ms. Bush," he clowned.

"You are so stupid," I said as I slowly sat on his lap while Ginuwine - "Pony" was playing. We started moving to the same rhythm.

Moaning, he said, "Baby, you feel so good."

"You feel better," I groaned.

We were so in sync with one another. He caressed my back and kissed and sucked my neck. I loved when he sucked my neck. He knew that always took me there. When the love song we made together ended, he carried me to the bed.

I was content and ready to go to sleep.

Sly kissed my forehead and asked if I was okay. I was more than okay. He kissed me and started massaging my big feet. They were extra swollen from all the walking I did earlier.

Sly said, "Baby, I love your feet.

They look just like little pig's feet."

"I know you are not busting on my feet because your feet look like ribs with burnt onion tips," I teased him.

We laughed. He sucked my big toe.

"Baby, it feels like a pacifier is in my mouth."

I told him to pacify these tits.

He said that's why he can't stand me.

We joked like that for a few more minutes then went to sleep.

Chapter 10
Home-Going Drama

The next day was the day of the funeral. I wasn't feeling to well and was sad. I kept telling myself that Grandma is in a better place.

Sly was being so helpful. He ironed my dress and helped Shaquan with his tie. He shocked me. I didn't know he knew how to tie a tie. The things you discover during a funeral. He fixed breakfast sandwiches—something quick but good. Anything I asked him to do, he did.

Shaquan made me smile when he said, "If you want to cry, Mommy, cry on me."

I told him that I love him and that he is mommy's number one baby.

My Big Boy was so supportive, and so was my big man. The two of them were making the day go as easy as possible.

My sister finally knocked on the door. Before we left, she and Sly sat in her car and smoked.

"Are y'all serious," I yelled. "Is this what the two of you came up with all by yourselves?"

"Stop hating," said Diamond.

"Hurry up," I said impatiently.

"I know you are not talking because we usually is waiting on your late ass," she replied.

I looked at the two of them, rolled my eyes, and shook my head.

Eventually they were done smoking.

"I hope that Sly didn't smoke too much because I don't want him driving like the Dukes of Hazzard. We don't need to be getting into any car accidents."

She said, "Sis, its real funny that you been weed free for eight months, but all the time when you was smoking and driving you never said or thought about any car accidents. You know, you are something else."

"Yes, I am, and so are you," I sassed.

In Sly's truck, all of our swag was on one thousand. We were grooving to Faith Evans and Mary J—my favorite female R&B artists. I promise you, nobody is messing with them two. We pulled up to my grandparents' house and saw that everybody was already there.

We greeted everybody. I kissed and hugged my parents. This was my mother's mom that we were burying. I asked my mom how she was holding up.

"Better than yesterday," she told me.

She asked how I was.

"We are going to get through this as a family," I said.

"That's my number one," my father responded.

He always treated me and my sis the same, but he and I had that firstborn daughter and father bond. My father wasn't as religious as my mother. In fact, he could care less about religion.

Church wasn't at the top of his list; however, he feared God.

When I was young, he would tell me that until I feared God, I was going to fear him. That's gangsta, isn't it? But that's real talk.

My uncle did a great job arranging the transportation. Everyone was in a limo and was able to chill, talk, and laugh. We anticipated a big funeral because Grandma was known all over the city of Philadelphia. A legend has gone.

The parking lot was full. Christ Deliverance was a mega church that seated ten thousand people. I have never seen so many cars parked in a church parking lot.

The family lined up and went inside the church. Diamond, Shaquan, Sly, and me went to view the body together. I heard Sly whisper something about keeping his promise. I tried to communicate that I believed him without saying a word.

We were seated, and the home-going service for Grandma began, but before Pastor Jones preached, Diamond shocked everyone and sang "I Love the Lord." No, she wasn't on the program, and to this day, I don't know how she got that off, but she did. And she sung under the anointing.

At one point, Sly started to cry.

I turned and asked, "Baby, you good?"

He shook his head. "Yeah, babe. I'm just feeling that feeling."

"What feeling," I asked.

Sly answered, "The ghost."

"The Holy Ghost," I asked.

He replied, "Yeah, that's what you call it."

I said okay, but wanted to ask Sly when he started feeling the Holy Spirit. This was his first time in church since he was ten years old. But I didn't go there. I just hoped he would get it together.

Then I started to feel something. No, it wasn't the Holy Ghost. It was contractions. They were bearable. I said to God, *Please, I know you work in mysterious ways, but this funeral is not the place for my water to break.*

Sly noticed that I wasn't feeling okay.

"Baby, is this too much for you?"

"No. I'm going to get through this service no matter what."

After the service was over, I couldn't count the number of people who came up to share condolences. Sly was there every step of the way. Some of the older people even recognized him from the projects. One lady felt she had to say something to me.

"Baby, how did you hook up with him," the eighty-something-year-old woman said. "Your grandma was such a good Christian woman. She would turn over in her grave if she knew that you were with him. His whole family is wicked. You have no business meddling with those kinds of people."

With my nose turned up I responded, "Thank you, ma'am. Please pray for me and him," I said in a nice but nasty manner.

I smirked as I walked away. I wanted to tell her she had no business meddling in my business. I was already considered a rebel, and I didn't want any trouble at Grandma's funeral. I wanted Grandma to be proud of her pretty girl.

Sly wanted to smoke a cigarette, so we went outside. A girl moved toward us, looking like she wanted to fight. Then Sly started looking real mean. This girl wasn't even dressed like she was at a funeral. She was wearing booty shorts with a tight black shirt. Her big gut was hanging out over her shorts. She was brown skinned, around five foot three, and she looked like she was about 215 pounds with a huge butt.

"Sly, you remember me," she declared.

Before he could say anything, I asked, "Who are you?"

She turned around and mooned us. There were ten names tattooed across her ass. She was pointing to Sly's name on it and said, "I'm Buf, the name slayer." She turned back around and pulled her shorts up and said, "I name him while you play him. She said what Twinkle you don't know about me?" I said obviously not and why are you here.

"My mom knew your grandma, and I wanted to pay my respects," she said, and then she straight told on Sly. "Sly told me he was going to be here with your ass. Yeah, he told me a couple weeks ago to stop calling him because he's about to marry you and that he is done with me. He's been ignoring my phone calls." She turned toward Sly. "Yeah, I just stepped on the church grounds to check your ass."

135

I said, "You ain't gonna do shit on these grounds."

By this time, some of my cousins are outside and ready to rumble. Diamond is standing right behind Buf, waiting for me to give her the signal. My sis was always ready, especially when it came to me.

"Yeah, you gonna marry this bitch," she asked Sly.

He told her to get out of here before she gets hurt.

"I ain't never going nowhere because your name is tattooed on my ass," ignorantly she responded while hollering.

"Along with nine other assholes," agitatedly I replied. "But I promise you one of those names is a chick."

"Twinkle, like I just said, you play him and I name him." That was her attempt at a comeback.

"Obviously, he played your dumb, desperate, zany ass," I said. "Get out of my face."

Right on cue, Diamond said, "Yo, Huf...Buf...whatever your name is I don't care. All I'm saying is that today is not the day to draw because you will get your ass beat. Then my initials will be tatted on your face with my fist and blade. So I'm asking you nicely to leave."

As she was walking away, she told Sly that he'd be back.

This chick "ass" was unbelievable. It was XL, and while she was walking away, it seemed like her ass never left.

Everyone started looking at Sly sideways. He apologized, but I was already upset because he was smoking on church grounds. Now this! To me, this was a clear sign that Grandma changed her mind and that she didn't like him anymore. My mind kept playing back to what that old lady said about Sly.

Sly had a black cloud hovering over him, and it seemed like when I was with him, the same cloud was hovering over me too. For so long, I thought those nasty chicks were the problem. I finally got the memo. Sly is the problem. I wanted to kick him in his balls. Buf wasn't blameless. I wanted to bash that chick's face in. Instead, I walked away from Sly. I left him standing there, disgusted and embarrassed.

He ran after me. "VP!" he called out. "Baby, I'm so sorry. I didn't know she was going to be here. Please, don't let her mess up this day. I'm done with all those girls, and I love you and only you. Please, baby, don't be mad at me. I'm sorry, and I'm sorry this happened to you, especially today."

I didn't say anything and kept walking.

"Isn't God a forgiving God?" he asked.

"Yes, but I'm not God."

"Babe, see, this is what she wants," he was pleading at this point. "She is miserable because I told her, and all the rest of them girls, that I was done with them because I love you. You don't deserve to be hurt. Twinkle, you don't deserve to cry. You deserve all my heart, not part of me and I'm ready to give the game up. You stuck by me for all these years, not nobody else, and I will never take that for granted again." Sly kissed me. "Baby, please believe me."

"I do believe you, but I'm still angry," I told him.

Because it was Grandma's funeral, I was trying my best to be good. I tried to look at the situation differently. If Sly wasn't here, I would be mad about that. But he was here supporting me.

All my older cousins was looking at him and shaking their head, and all my younger cousins wanted to beat Buf's ass. We went to the burial then returned to the church. I saw cousins I hadn't seen in years. While talking with my cousin Pamela, we discovered she had married and divorced Sly's first cousin James. They had three beautiful girls together. She said that my baby is going to be her daughter's cousin on both sides. We were so amazed at that.

Pam told me that Sly's family is a piece of work. She told me how her ex stole her BMW and sold it for $25 that he spent on drugs. She said she been through so much with James.

Pam was a registered nurse and made good money. She was about Sly's age. She told me that her brother, my cousin Brian, used to hang close with Sly when they were younger. Sly was buck wild then. Brian used to be in love with Sly's sister Dorian.

"Twinkle," she said, with a puzzled look. "I don't know what it is that attracts us to that family."

"Cuz, me neither."

She wished us the best. She also warned me that their family had more tricks than Kiddie City, so I should be careful.

"Cuz," Pam reiterated, "I know you're pregnant, but don't

give him your whole heart because he might break it."

We hugged and kissed and exchanged numbers.

It seemed like everybody knew Sly's family, and nobody had anything good to say about them.

The funeral, burial, and repast made for a long day. When it was over, the majority of the family went back to my grandparent's house, but Shaquan, Sly, Diamond, and I went home.

I started feeling crampy again, but I was happy that I didn't have the baby at the funeral. I just wanted to lie down.

I told Sly that our baby was coming this week. I could just feel it. Truthfully, I was ready. I was tired of my feet being swollen, and I was tired of carrying this big baby in this small space. I was tired of sharing my body, and I wanted my body back to myself.

Chapter 11
Suspect

Come Saturday, Sly was antsy. I kept looking at him like what's wrong. Maybe he was nervous because I was due any day.

"Babe, let's go to the park so we can try to walk this baby out and so Shaquan can run around for a few," he suggested.

"Okay," I agreed. My Big Boy was so excited that we were going to the park.

"Mommy, can I ride my bike?" he asked.

"Sure."

Sly packed lunch and put Big Boy's bike in the truck. We drove to the park where we walked and we talked for a while. I finally had to tell Sly that I was tired and I have to sit down.

He brought out the blankets, cooler, and the battery-operated radio. I turned it on and my boy Busta's joint was on "Put Your Hands Where My Eyes Can See." Sly told me to drink a lot of water and eat some of the fruit.

I looked at this dude like; don't tell me what to do. I sat down in a shaded area and rested. I drank bottled water, snacked on some pineapples and strawberries, and listened to the radio while I read a book.

Sly and Big Boy chased the ducks. Sly and Big Boy looked like two big kids chasing after them. You should have seen the ducks running away. It was so funny. Shaquan got hungry, so they came back and ate their sandwiches. We laughed and danced and had a lot of fun.

Big Boy asked if he could ride his bike.

"Yeah, but make sure you don't go too far and stay where I can see you."

While he was riding his bike, Sly wanted to play trouble.

"Where did you find this game at? I didn't even know that trouble was still out," I admitted. "What's next, Sly? Candy land?"

"Something is really wrong with you," Sly laughed.

We played trouble five times, and Sly won every game. He said that he has the luck of the Irish.

"You're lucky because this is a whack-ass game," I responded. "Let's play let's go home. I'm hot, I'm done eating, and I rather be in my central air. It feels like Africa out here."

"I just wanted you to get dressed and for you to do your hair because you were looking a mess," Sly said sarcastically. "I knew that the only way you would get yourself together was if we were going somewhere. Don't you feel better now because you got your grown and sexy look on?"

I replied with confidence. "I'm always sexy." I continued, "What you trying to say Sly? I asked, while getting smart with him. You are not that thoughtful, your ass is crafty. What's really going on with you? Don't think I haven't noticed you been acting suspect all morning."

"Babe, I'm good," he replied.

"Okay, but what you do in the dark will come to the light."

Sly added, "The only thing that is coming out of the dark is my baby."

"Okay, Sly, and again that was so corny."

He accused me of always trying to diss somebody. I told him I wasn't trying to diss him. I was just telling the truth.

"You cranky b—," he uttered.

"Sly, I want you to say it, As a matter of fact, I dare you to. Cranky what, Sly?"

"Cranky baby mom," he said with a laugh.

"Oh! That's what I thought."

We agreed to leave after Shaquan came back around. Sly started packing. I saw him checking messages on his phone and I started to get pissed off. I knew he was up to something.

Here we go with the reindeer games. Sly thinks that I'm really stupid.

Big Boy came back, and I told him it was time to go. He yelled, "One more time, Mommy?"

"Go ahead, son." How could I say no.

I looked at Sly with my lips perched sideways. *What's he up to?* Sly walked over and asked if I was ready.

"Yeah. Shaquan wanted to ride around the park one more time."

When Big Boy turned to come back, Sly helped me up and folded the blankets.

"Baby, I really do love you."

"Sly, you are sounding real suspect right now, and I don't

believe a word your saying."

"Well, frisk me then, baby mom."

"Who was you talking to on the phone?" Straightforwardly I asked.

"Nobody, I was listening to my messages."

I kept asking questions, "Who left you a message?"

"Nobody," he proclaimed. "I was checking on something."

"What was you checking on, Sly?"

"Baby mom, simmer down, I can't wait until you have this baby because you are too emotional."

"Don't try to blame my pregnancy and put this on me when I clearly saw you on your phone. All day you've been real antsy, like you're nervous about something. It got to the point you were making me nervous. And now my investigating antennas are up."

"Those Deer Antlers never go down," he responded.

"All right, Sly, you got that off."

Out of nowhere, Sly blurted, "It's around five thirty."

"I didn't ask you what time it is. What, you have somewhere to go?"

He said, "Nah."

We started walking to the truck because Shaquan had returned. I sat in the truck while Sly put Shaquan's bike in the back. I told Shaquan to make sure his seat belt was on.

When I got settled at home, I called my sister. We talked for a few; then I said, "Sis Sly has been acting real suspect."

"That's because he is," Diamond replied.

"Thanks, sis, for the encouragement," I said sarcastically.

"I was just telling you what you already know."

I told her that I will talk to her later because I wasn't feeling the love from her. She told me not to get an attitude with her for saying what I already know.

"Hey," she said. "What did you want me to tell you?"

"You know what, I can't. Your mouth and Sly's suspicious behavior are too much." Then I banged on her.

Sly and Big Boy were in the living room playing chess while I was in my bedroom watching TV. The doorbell rang.

I wondered, "Who is at the door and why?"

Sly yelled, "VP, get the door."

"Why," I shouted back, "when you are in the living room."

"Just get the damn door," he ordered.

I walked into the living room and said, "Don't be cussing in front of my son, negro."

Sly apologized to Shaquan.

"It's okay, Sly, because I'm going to beat your ass in chess," Shaquan said.

"Shaquan," I said, "you have one more time, and I promise you I'm going to beat your little ass."

As I walked back to my room, I muttered, "Both of y'all are getting on my darn nerves. As a matter of fact, everybody is!"

I heard them both chuckle.

"So, VP, how you just not going to answer the door," Sly asked?

I walked back to the bedroom and yelled, "Because I can," then slammed the door and laid back down.

Sly knocked on the door.

"What?"

"Babe," he said as he peeped from behind the door. "You got a FedEx package."

"I didn't order anything, and then it occurred to me what was going on. Oh, I get it. You ordered something. What did you order, Sly?"

"Nothing," he said as he laid the package next to me and shut the door as he went back into the living room.

I was so disgusted. My name was on the package, but I didn't order anything. So I walked in the living room.

"Sly, why don't you open your package?"

"Why?" he asked. "Do you think it's going to blow up?"

"Maybe, you've been acting suspicious all day, and now I receive a package that I know nothing about."

"Well, I'm not opening it," he said.

I threw the package in the trash. Sly wasn't going to blow me and my son up. I walked back into my bedroom and laid down and watched TV. Sly came and knocked on my door.

"Babe, I will open the package," he replied.

I told him to give me one minute and called my sister.

"I received a strange package," I told her in a rushed whisper. "If something happens to me and Big Boy, Sly's responsible."

"Call me as soon as you open it," Diamond said. At times my sister can be just so lackadaisical.

I told her, "I'm not opening it, Sly is. But I will call you back. If I don't call back within fifteen minutes, you already know what to do."

We hung up. I walked back into the living room and told Shaquan to come and sit on Mommy's lap while Sly opened the package.

It was a cream and gold, Louis Vuitton bag, and it was sharp.

"Babe, thank you." I was so happy, I put on the Mary J. / Keith Murray "Be Happy" remix CD and started dancing a little. I kinda felt a bit silly about the way I was thinking earlier. But who cares, even y'all thought something crazy was about to pop off. Don't judge me.

A while ago, I was online and showed Sly the bag. I wanted it, but he acted like he wasn't paying attention.

"You are always full of surprises," I said. All I could do was smile.

"Do you like it?" Sly asked.

Still smiling, I said, "I love it!"

"I love you, and I love Shaquan," he said.

I couldn't hold back the tears. I was so happy that I gave Sly a big hug and kiss. I gave Shaquan a big kiss too. I thanked him again then went into my room to call Diamond.

"Guess what!"

She said, "What?"

"Sly got me that Louis Vuitton bag that I wanted."

"Oh, that was the reason why he was acting suspect," she asked.

"Yes. I almost told him off," I giggled. "Thank God I didn't."

"Even if you did tell him off," Diamond snapped. "It just would have been for all the times that he didn't get caught."

"Damn, sis," I said. "Can't you just enjoy the moment?"

"I'm enjoying it, sis."

"Okay, I'm sensing that you are busy," I told her.

"I was on my way out," she responded.

I just hung up on her. Diamond came past for a surprise visit around nine that night. I knew she was coming over because she was curious. Plus she didn't appreciate me bangin' on her.

"Okay, Sly," she said while checking out the bag. "I see you trying. Sis, the bag is suga' sharp!"

Sly and Diamond went outside to smoke. Those two had a weird relationship, but they were cool. When they came back in, Diamond said she was going to watch Shaquan tonight so me and Sly can chill.

I told her that me and Sly didn't have anything planned.

"I bought my neph some outfits and books," she said. "And besides, I'm trying to stay out of trouble tonight."

Diamond loved her nephew. He was her road dog. I went into Big Boy's room to pack his overnight bag. I heard Sly and my sister whispering. I wondered why they would be whispering and almost said something to them both, but I knew in my heart that my sister was not shady. Now Sly, on the other hand—I couldn't trust him as far as I could throw him. I knew that buffoon was shady, but I trusted my sister. We never would cross that line and sleep with each other's man. We loved and respected one another.

After Big Boy's bag was packed, he and I walked in the living room. Sly and Diamond had a look on their face like they were hiding something, but I wasn't going to trip because I know my sister. Eventually she would tell me what the hell was going on. So I kind of shook it off. I'm pregnant and emotional.

I thought, *Stop trippin', Twinkle. That's you're li'l sis, and things are not what they look like.*

Big Boy gave me a hug and a kiss, my sis told me that she will see me later, and they were gone.

Sly asked, "Baby, you hungry?"

"Yeah," I replied. "What are you fixing?"

"I have a taste for Chinese," he said.

I replied, "That sounds good."

Sly asked, "Baby, what do you want?"

I responded, "Chicken lo mein, shrimp fried rice, a large lemonade, and don't forget the ice."

Then Sly responded rhyming back, "I have a taste for some shrimp lo mein, chicken fried rice, a large lemonade, and they better have my damn ice."

He said, "Hey!" He started snappin' his fingers and boppin'

his head. That dude was happy that he was about to eat, and he had a moment.

I called the order in and told Sly it will be ready in fifteen minutes.

He responded, "Okay, sweetheart."

Sweetheart? That's new.

I went into the bedroom to lay down; then Sly asked if I would pick up the food.

"No, did you forget that I'm the one pregnant here."

"I know, but I'm not feeling good," he said.

"Just a minute ago you was boppin' and snappin'. Now, all of a sudden, you don't feel good. Okay, Sly! What's going on?"

"Nothing, baby," he smiled.

"Negro, you are about to get caught, I promise you. All day you been acting suspicious."

"Babe, I was acting like that because I was trying to track when the bag was going to arrive. That's why I was checking my messages at the park," he explained. "Babe, I know I did a lot of shit, but I changed. The only thing I want to see is you're Colgates."

I frowned up my face. "My Colgates?"

"Yes, your teeth, baby, from smiling," he replied.

"Oh! My pearly whites," I responded.

"That's a whole lot of smiling," I said.

"I know, baby, and you deserve it."

"You damn skippy I deserve it," I said.

"So, baby, will you get the Chinese food for us," he asked.

"No! You get it because, all of a sudden, I don't feel very well."

He said, "Babe, stop playing."

Reluctantly I said, "Okay. Give me the money."

Sly put his hand out. I snatched the money. He said all that good shit, so I decided to test him.

As I drove to the restaurant, I figured he couldn't do too much at my house any way. He just bought me a thousand-dollar bag. It was the bag that I really wanted. We spent the day at the park. Maybe he is really tired.

At the restaurant, the lady told me Sly called and added chicken wings, so I had to wait. I was so disgusted. Here I am, eight months pregnant, I didn't want to get the food in the first place, and now I have to wait because Sly decides to add to the order after it was called in.

I called Sly, and he didn't pick up the phone. Maybe he was in the bathroom. He wouldn't have left. I called back, and he still didn't answer. *He'll call me back*, I thought. I waited for the food for what felt like thirty minutes.

I drove home, but Sly still hadn't called me back, and I was mad.

"What if my water broke or what if something happened to me?" I raised the question out loud in the car. "He wouldn't know because he is not picking up the damn phone or calling me back. When I get home, I'm going to cuss his asinine ass out. I ain't no fool."

When I arrived back home, I was ready to go in Sly's mouth. When I opened the door, "Butta Love" by Next was playing, and there were lit candles everywhere. The lights were dim, all my slow jams were playing, and there were seven bouquets of posies around the apartment. Sly knew that seven is my favorite number. There were yellow tulips, orchids, irises, lilacs, roses, sunflowers, and lilies.

Sly took the food from me and put it in the kitchen.

He said, "I just wanted to surprise you. I love you. I ran your bath. Tonight, I want you to relax."

"What is the occasion?" I asked.

He answered, "The occasion is love, and we are celebrating love, true love, tonight."

"That's what's up."

When I went into the bathroom, rose petals were sprinkled on the floor. There were more bouquets of flowers. Everything was so beautiful.

I couldn't figure out where he hid all the flowers. Wherever they were hidden, he planned this evening nicely. Sly did it big, and I was happy and surprised. He had filled my day with happy surprises.

I was in the tub for about fifteen minutes when Sly came in and told me not to go swimming because he didn't want the food to get cold.

"I know, honey, but I don't mind heating my food in the

microwave. That is your pet peeve, not mine."

"VP," he replied, "you just can't help yourself. You always have something to say."

"And that is why you love me. Since you are in here monitoring me, can you help me up?"

So Sly helped me out of the tub, and I dried off, oiled up, and put on some sweet perfume and some lip sauce. (Yes you read it right I call it sauce not gloss). I pinned my hair up really cute and put on something sexy but comfortable.

I sat down at the kitchen table to my already-made plate. Sly was sitting down waiting for me. He would never start eating without me. Why he waited, I don't know. Sly had a lot of old-school ways.

I asked him, "Honey, is this the reason why you've been so antsy today?"

He responded, "If you say so."

Sly and I both were hungry, and we really didn't like to talk much while we were eating. We liked to enjoy our food. When I was just about done, he said, "Lisa."

Sly doesn't call me Lisa often so when he called me by my real name, I knew it was something serious. I responded, "*Lisa!* Shawn, you must be about to tell me something." I gave him my serious look.

He took a deep breath and said, "I never felt this way with any woman before. I'm the boy Sly. I don't chase women. I replace them, but there is no replacement when it comes to you."

I wanted to say something smart, but I knew that Sly was serious, and this wasn't the time. He got down on one knee and said, "Lisa Renee Valentine, a.k.a. Twinkle, will you marry me?"

"Sly! Yes!"

He pulled out the ring and it was bling blingin'. It was beautiful. All I could do is cry.

Sly hugged me, and we held each other tight. "VP, this ring is six carats—a carat representing each year we've been together."

Now I knew why him and Diamond were whispering and why she suddenly asked to watch Big Boy. Everything made sense. I couldn't do anything but cry tears of joy.

"I'm ready to settle down, and I want to be your husband. I made a promise to Grandma, and, baby, I'm going to keep it."

That night, I laid in his arms all night in awe. Words could not explain how I was truly feeling inside. All I can say, I was truly happy.

In the morning, I started having contractions, and they were for real. I called the doctor. The doctor asked did my water break? I told him no. He told me to wait but if the contractions begin to get closer then give him a call back.

Sly tried to make me comfortable, but it wasn't working. After an hour, I called the doctor back. The contractions were close enough, so he told me to come in. Sly had already prepared my hospital bag, and he drove me to the hospital, I was immediately put in a room. I had dilated six centimeters, but my water had not broken.

The doctor eventually arrived.

"Lisa," he announced, "you are going to have a baby today."

The doctor broke my water, and the labor pains got worse. Sly encouraged me the entire time. It got to the point where I asked for an epidural. I tried to hold out, but this drug is legal. So why not! They called the anesthesiologist, and she gave me the epidural. That needle was long, but I didn't care because I knew it was going to make me feel better.

After a few minutes, the contractions did not hurt as much. I asked Sly to call my sister and my parents. He had to leave out of the hospital to call them because he couldn't use his cell phone inside.

As I was laying in the bed, I remembered my prayer after my Grandma died. I ask God if he would bless me with a healthy girl. I needed my baby to remind me that Grandma was still here with me.

I prayed again. *Father, today is the big day and I pray that you will grant this prayer in Jesus's name, amen.* I heard Grandma in my spirit saying call unto him and he will answer. When I heard that, I was certain that I was having a baby girl. God would not disappoint me twice.

I called Kay from my hospital room phone to tell her that I am having the baby. She said she would call everybody.

Sly came back. "VP, you good?"

"Sly, if I tell you no, what are you really going to do?"

"Yeah," he smiled. "You good."

Diamond and Big Boy came into my room. My son was so happy; he couldn't wait for his brother or sister to get here. The joy in his eyes was priceless.

Now everybody was at the hospital: Diamond, Big Boy, my parents, Kay, C, Ree, Bertha, and Sly. The energy was positive and joyful.

The doctor came in to check me and cleared the room. I didn't want them to see my moneymaker anyway.

The refined and proper doctor said, "You are nine and a half centimeters. You are almost there. In a few minutes you will be able to start pushing. I am going to go get the nurse."

I got really close to my doctor over the months, and I really liked him. He was concerned about my well-being, and he didn't treat me like I was a statistic.

Still excited, everyone came back into the room. It seemed like they all noticed my engagement ring at the same time, probably because Sly told them when they were in the hallway.

Kay spoke first. "Damn, Sly, you really did your thing and took your time when you picked out my girl's ring. I still don't like you, but if my girl is happy, then so am I."

Then C said, "Sly, I always knew you were a good guy."

"Yeah, it had to be some good in you if you stayed with Twinkle's crazy ass for all these years," Bertha added.

Ree nudged him. "Sly, don't mess up. We understand that nobody's perfect, but just remain consistent."

"I will, Ree," Sly confessed with sincerity.

"Okay, everybody! Thank you, but Sly is not the focus here. It's me and the baby. Thank you."

Just then the nurse walked in, and she said it was time. Everyone except Sly got out of dodge.

Sly looked at me. "You ready, baby?"

"Yeah, it's now or never."

He kissed me and said, "Let's do this."

I looked at the clock. It was 3:15 p.m. I whispered, "God, I'm about to push my baby girl out. Thank you in advance for her."

I smiled and started pushing. I pushed and I pushed. The magnitude of the contractions felt life-taking. I was pushing so hard that my eyelids flipped up. I wanted this baby out. Every time the nurse said push, I gave it all I had.

Sly bent down to pick something up from the floor.

In a soft tone, I heard his deep but embarrassed voice say, "Babe, some of your micro braids are on floor."

"In disgust I said, what do you want me to do, Sly!" It really wasn't a question.

The nurse interrupting our conversation said stop pushing, "I see the head."

The doctor interjected, "This is going to be a big one." In order to prevent any tearing, he started to stretch me.

Sly whispered in my ear, "He better stop playing with my wife's pussy like that." He winked.

I wanted to laugh, but I was in so much pain that all I could do was shake my head. I kept pushing and stopping until the doctor said, "Now! Push hard."

I did, and I heard my baby cry. Before I could ask, the doctor said, "It's a girl."

I cried, "Thank you, Jesus, for answering my prayer and bringing my Grandma back to me."

The time of her arrival was 4:03 p.m.

They cleaned her off and gave her to me. She was nine pounds, seven ounces and twenty-one inches long. It was August 10, 2000.

She was big and beautiful, just like me, with a head full of straight, black hair. While I was holding her, Sly was crying.

He asked, "What are we going to name her?"

With all the pride I could muster, I said, "Fannie Esther."

"Babe, I know you love and miss Grandma. I understand that you are going through something right now, but we are not naming our baby after your grandma."

I whined, "Please, baby."

"Twinkle," Sly responded, "my baby, our baby is the upgrade version of Grandma. Therefore, she needs an upgraded name, like a twenty-first–century name."

I laughed and said, "Okay, baby, what about Anisa Queen Dior?"

"That's cute."

"Sly," I asked, "did you really think that I was going to name her Fannie Esther?"

We both laughed.

"Girl, you play too much, and you never stop."

"That's why you love me."

Sly kissed me on my forehead, "Babe, I do."

All my family and friends came in. Big Boy rushed to our side and kept kissing his sister. "Thank you, God," he said, "for answering my prayers. Now I have a little sister."

I knew that he was going to be a good big brother. I prayed that they would always be close just like me and my sister.

"My niece looks like Sly," Kay implied.

"You can't tell who she looks like because she's been in water for nine months," I said.

"Stop hatin' and face reality that she has Sly's mean-looking face," Kay said, but quickly added, "She's cute though."

I told Kay, "Go somewhere."

She replied, "She's a baby with an attitude. Poor thing didn't have too much of a choice. She is you and Sly combined in one."

"Babe," Sly spoke up, "our baby does look like me."

"No, she doesn't."

Sly didn't back down. "Yes, she does. The only features she has of yours is your complexion and those fat feet looking like young pig feet."

"Whatever, Sly. My feet are cute unlike your slave-like, ugly feet. Looking like you had been walking in Huntington Park barefoot."

"I think that she's gonna get darker because she has little dark spots on her back," Sly said. "I think that my dark skin gene is trying to take over."

"Never that," I said. "And you see who won."

He said, "Yeah, you, baby. I'm going to nickname her CC standing for Chocolate Chip."

Can you tell Sly likes to eat? My nickname is vanilla pound cake and baby girl's is chocolate chip, which I thought was cute. Finally, our baby girl is here.

The doctor explained that the spots on Anisa's back are Mongolian spots. He said the spots are common among darker-skinned people. They are noncancerous and will probably go away. Thank God because they looked like bruises.

I couldn't stop staring at Anisa and Big Boy. Through it all, God still saw fit to bless my womb. I couldn't stop kissing her. Big Boy was so excited that his little sister was finally here.

"Mommy, can I hold her?"

Although Shaquan was six, I knew he would not be careless with her. He prayed for her and Sly was sitting right there next to him in case something did go wrong.

Sly handed Anisa to Shaquan. His eyes got bright, and his smile got even bigger than it already was. I felt like my kids and I were going to be all right. I had two healthy children, and Sly just proposed to me. God had answered my prayers along with Big Boy's. Sly was trying to be domesticated. I was so overjoyed. I felt like I was dreaming. Everything was too good to be true. Grandma would always tell me everything was gonna be all right. I couldn't stop smiling.

Eventually they put me in another room. Everybody went home, and it was just me and baby girl. Although my baby was beautiful, I wasn't feeling the frown mark between her eyebrows. I had to be honest; she did have Sly's mean-looking face. My baby had no reason to look mean; she is innocent and pure.

I said to her, "Anisa Queen Dior Valentine, you will not grow up with a mean look. You will be happy, and you will be free."

I prayed and asked God to change Anisa's countenance and for her to look happy and for her to be happy. I was told that our eyes are the windows to our soul. If you look crazy, you are crazy. Eyes don't lie.

I'm not saying that my baby was crazy, but I had enough knowledge to know that we all are born into sin and shaped into iniquity. If I could help it, through my prayers, my baby was not going to be shaped in iniquity.

Anisa needed a chance to live life the way God intended for her. See, Sly was old, and he is who he is, but my baby was my baby. I wasn't going to let life cheat her out her happiness at an early age or any age.

I knew Sly lived an angry life, and that's why his face looked so mean. It's funny, that mean look is what attracted me to him at first, but now, seeing that same look on my baby's face gave me a different feeling.

As I drifted to sleep, I felt this was the beginning of something new, something deeper than just my baby.

Around nine in the morning, Diamond woke me. I had been up every few hours because I was breast feeding. So when I finally got some sleep, I went in—knocked out and sleeping good.

"Sis," I heard her say, "wake up, sis."

She knew not to get too close because I might punch her by mistake.

"Diamond," I said with much attitude, "why are you here so early?"

"I have to go to work, unlike you," she snapped, "and I wanted to see my niece before I went."

"Well, excuse me."

My sister was so excited about her niece. That is the only reason why I didn't tell her off the way I really wanted. Of course she was making her jokes, saying, "Sis, you are going to have to hit the gym hard because your chin is looking like Ms. Melody in the place to be."

Double chin and all. Ms. Melody is cute, and I damn sure is.

I came back by saying, "You're looking like Missy before she lost her weight. Now what?"

"Ooh! Sis, you got that one off, and you lucky you just had my niece 'cause I would fight you."

We started laughing. Diamond was always busting on somebody. She just couldn't help it. She would bust by mistake; it was just in her DNA.

She would oftentimes say that the reason why she was so funny is because she told the truth. There's always some truth in a joke, right?

Chapter 12
Real Talk

"Sis?" she said, suddenly becoming serious. "Do you think Sly is really serious this time around? I see your six-carat rock, but what good is a rock without a ceremony?"

"You're right," I told her. "That's why I'm taking it nice and slow."

"I know. That's what got you here—you and Sly's slow motion." Her jokes were back on.

"I don't know if it was our slow motion or if it was that Luke-type thug lovin' on some don't-stop-get-it-get-it type shit," I admitted.

"Yo sis, what is really wrong with you?"

"If it ain't rough, then it ain't right," I said.

We laughed.

"You're nasty for real, sis," Diamond said as she shook her head.

"Like you ain't," I pointed out. "You just didn't get caught."

"Because I'm boss. But real rap." Diamond wasn't going to let me get away without answering her question. "Do you think Sly is going to change?"

"Do you?" I asked. "Because you are the one asking me all the questions. What do you want me to do? Do you want me to leave him now? Sly has been around this long. Why would he leave now? What do you think, since you know it all?"

"All I'm saying is that now you have two kids, and I don't need a tribe of nieces and nephews from you and Sly," she stated. "Either he is going to marry you and do it right or keep it moving. You and your kids deserve the best. Your kids don't need to be seeing instability and drama. We both know that Sly is good for fourteen days, and then he'll be right back to the malarkey. Sly can only do what you allow him to do. Stop allowing it."

In my heart, I knew Diamond was saying all of this because she wasn't feeling Sly. Even though he proposed to me, it was all a front in her eyes.

"Diamond, why don't you like Sly?"

"Because his lips are still black," she replied.

When we were young, my favorite cousin, Presheous, told us to never trust people with black lips because they lie. When I say Diamond and I lived by that, we lived by that. But we made exceptions when it came to our men.

"I try because I know how much you love him, but let's call a spade by a spade," Diamond continued. "It is what it is."

Inside, I knew she was telling me right. Diamond loved me and her niece and nephew with all of her heart. I loved her back in the same measure—maybe a little more because I was the oldest and took care of her when we were kids. There was nothing that she couldn't ask or tell me because she had that sister right. It seemed like we could read each other's mind to the point she would tell me to get out of her mind. We would wonder if other sisters had that kind of connection.

Diamond, now eyeball to eyeball with me, asked "What's wrong with you?"

"I'm good," I answered.

"Yeah, you're good, but I know that something's bothering you."

"Well, since you know so much, what's bothering me?" I asked?

"That frown mark on Anisa face is bothering you," Diamond addressed.

"Wow! This is so spooky. How do we do this?"

She replied, "It's the sister bond. I know that you're thinking about somehow getting rid of it, but what I can't figure out is how."

"I prayed about it," I acknowledged.

"Sis, you've been praying a lot lately, which is unlike you. On the other hand, I take Jesus wherever I go. If I'm about to rob somebody, Jesus is there. When I'm pimpin' these dumb ibexes, Jesus is still there. What they say, he sticks closer to you than a brother. Sis, some of the things I be doing you can't come, but Jesus can. I pray all the time. When I'm copin', I'm asking Jesus, 'Please don't let me get caught.' And when I'm hustling, I pray again, 'Jesus, please don't let me get caught.' And Jesus be answering me because he knows my heart."

"Jesus also knows that your heart can wickedly deceive you

too," I said. "And, sis, you are being deceived."

"Here we go with the criticism," Diamond replied. "You been clean for nine months and you done prayed to Jesus maybe five times and read a pentastich of Psalms maybe seven times and now you quoting Scriptures."

"Sis," I responded, "it's constructive criticism because I don't want anything to happen to you while you are out there doing your thing."

"It's not because I told you, I take Jesus with me everywhere I go. I'm not playing, sis," said Diamond.

"Okay," I answered.

"Back to you," she said.

"Yes, back to me because you just had a moment."

"Yeah, I did. I had to shout Jesus out early because I'm not innocent, but I'm trying to live holy."

"Okay, sis," I sniggered. "You go right ahead and do that and let me know how you make out."

"You have a lot of jokes this morning laying on this hospital bed."

"Okay, but back to what I was saying before you decided to give God praise in your ghetto way. What I came up with is anointing the frown mark with the blessed oil Grandma gave me some time ago."

Diamond replied, "Sis, are you serious?"

"Yes."

She said, "I will never put that stuff on my forehead."

"Oh, Ms. Taking-Jesus-Everywhere-You-Go won't anoint yourself."

Grandma gave all of us a bottle one Christmas with some ChapStick and $50.

"That was like four years ago," Diamond said. "You still have that oil?"

"Yeah, what did you do with yours?"

Diamond responded, "Girl, one day I was about to fry some chicken and I didn't have any more oil. I was too tired to go to the store, so I used that big bottle of oil to fry the chicken, and that was the best chicken I've ever fried. The olive oil was on some other good stuff."

"So you used it as cooking oil, Diamond?"

"How would I look putting that stuff on my forehead every day?" she asked.

"Well, look, if Grandma gave it to us, it must have some power and significance to it. Since I still have mine, I'm going to use it now, and I might just anoint myself too."

"Well, you go ahead and do that and look all greasy on the forehead and smelling like salad dressing," Diamond said. "I've got to go to work. She told me that she loved me and she'd be back tomorrow."

"I'll be discharged tomorrow. I'll keep you posted," I told her.

"Holla," she said as she left.

A few minutes later, I heard someone humming in the

hallway and sounding real crazy. I said to myself, "I wish they would shut the hell up." As the humming got louder, the source of the noise entered my room. It was my favorite cousin Presheous, also known as Pricy. I haven't seen her in about a year.

She didn't live far, but she was a crackhead and stayed away for long periods of time. When she came through, she was grotesque, witty, jittery, and crazier than a flip flop. Presheous was a straight basket case—she knew it and didn't care. She was always honest about her habit. There was a time when I would leave my money out when she came over just to test her. She never stole from me, so we were always good. She didn't really want to be a smoker; she just had a bad monkey on her back because she encountered a lot of hurt in her childhood.

Presheous was eight years older than me. She used to braid my hair when I was a little girl and into my adult years. When I tried to pay her, she would never take it. She preferred for me to take her to the mall and buy her something. My cousin was fly in her own way. She had an upfront presence, was street smart, would read anybody, and would not bite her tongue. Sometimes she would blurt things out, not even realizing what she was saying. I always paid attention to her because at any given moment she was going to call yours, hers, somebody's situation out.

The first thing Pricy said was where is Sly?

I was thinking the same thing because I hadn't seen him, and he had not called in a while. I wasn't about to call him because he knew where I was at.

"I don't know," I told her.

"Okay, where's the baby because I know she is here?"

I called the nurse's station and asked if they could bring my daughter down.

"You and Sly is not going to last," Pricy said.

"Yes, we are," I demanded.

"Where is he at?" she asked again.

I asked, "What does that have to do with Sly not being here?"

"Twinkle, I know my peoples."

Pricy's peoples were drug addicts and prostitutes because that's what she was, but through all of that, she still loved God. Nobody could tell me differently.

When Pricy was around ten years old, she accepted Christ as her personal Savior; however, her mom—my Aunt Hortez—didn't believe in God. It was like she hated God at that time. When Pricy was around twelve, she was praying out loud and was asking God to save her mom because she didn't want her mom to go to hell. Her mom overheard her and started beating Pricy with a broom so bad that the broom broke. Then she got the iron cord and beat her so bad that she started bleeding. Then Aunt Hortez told Pricy she wouldn't be able to live with her no more because she didn't believe in God.

Pricy was hurt and scared and called my grandma. She lived with Grandma until she was eighteen. But Grandma had some neighbors behind her who smoked crack. Pricy hooked up with them when she was thirteen and has been hooked on crack ever since. She went to church faithfully because that is all Grandma did, but Pricy couldn't overcome her habit.

By the time she was seventeen, Pricy had started disappearing, skipping school, and had stolen money from Grandma's purse. Aunt Hortez did some investigating and found out what was going on. She blamed herself.

The guilt drove Aunt Hortez to get saved. She talked to Pricy about rehab and rededicating her life back to God, but Pricy said she will never serve the same God that she serves.

Aunt Hortez never told Pricy she was sorry, she acted as if it didn't happen. But we all know the reason Pricy moved in with Grandma. As we got older, Pricy would sometimes ask me how can someone who says they love Jesus go to church and speak in tongues but can't admit they're wrong. Act as if they never did bad things, and never say sorry. She continued to say, "I am so sick of people that have a form of godliness but deny the power thereof."

Pricy started calling her mother a Pharisee and would say, "I'm a crackhead because crack is what I do."

Out of all my cousins, she knew the Bible the best because my Grandma had her for six years. I would listen to Pricy because I loved her and understood her hurt. She was my favorite cousin because she always treated me the best. So I didn't care what she did. I was always concerned about her when she would disappear, but I knew she knew how to take care of herself.

The nurse finally brought Anisa to the room.

"Ill! She got Sly's frown."

"I know, Pricy," I said with an attitude. "But she looks better than you."

"I didn't mean for it to come out like that, but I wasn't expecting to see his face on her face."

"She will be good," I said.

Then Pricy had the audacity to say, "Twinkle, it's time for you to start praying and to get your life together."

"When are you going to start praying and stop smoking crack?" I fired back at her.

"Twinkle, you have always been my favorite cousin, and I don't want you to wind up like me. We don't need no more crackheads in the family."

"Why weren't you at Grandma's funeral," I asked, changing the subject.

"I just couldn't do it," she said. "That's why I rushed to the hospital as soon as I heard you had the baby. I felt like I owed you and Grandma that."

"So you are never going to step foot in a church again, huh?"

"Only if God himself come down from heaven," Pricy said.

"I know what Auntie did to you was dead wrong, but in order for you to kick this habit, you must let that hurt go," I said. "Can't you see that she hurt you and now you are hurting yourself as a result? And I hate to see you like this. Just like you don't want me to be a crackhead, how much more do you think that I don't want you to be one? Your worth is so much more than a blow job and a trick."

"Twinkle, you know why you are my favorite cousin?" she asked.

"No."

Pricy never missed a beat. "Because what I see and know that you have inside of you, I always wanted and that is your strength. You were always strong. No matter what happened to you in life, you always weathered it."

"Pricy, do you know why you are my favorite cousin?"

Pricy replied, "No."

"You are crazier than a bed bug, and you never cared how much people talked about you," I said. "And what you don't know is that you are stronger than what you think. You still did you and you never had to lie or front for nobody. In my heart I know that you are tired of the streets. The simple fact that you are here lets me know that you are getting tired."

"Yes, I'm getting tired. Twinkle, the game never changes. The only thing that changes is the age. What I was doing at thirteen, I'm doing the same thing now at thirty-three."

We had a moment of silence, deep in thought.

I was thinking that it was time for me to change for the better, to take baby steps toward improvement. I have a little girl now. Do I really want her to cry and go through emotional turmoil, mental anguish, and physical abuse? My baby didn't deserve that life. If God granted me my prayer concerning Anisa, then I should do my best and raise her in a loving and peaceful environment. I just didn't know how to begin.

Pricy stayed at the hospital after visiting hours ended. She really didn't want to leave. I think she was feeling that as long as she was with me, she wasn't going to smoke.

I broke down and called Sly three times while Pricy was with me, but he didn't pick up. I didn't bother to leave any messages because I was beginning to feel fed up. R. Kelly ain't neva lie. My focus now was on Big Boy and Baby Girl.

Pricy saw the hurt in my eyes.

"Twinkle, now is the time for you to be the best mother for your kids. Shaquan is getting older, and you don't want him growing up to be a womanizer, abuser, or making sorry-ass excuses for his wrong," she told me.

"You are right," I said, "but I just don't know how to begin because I genuinely love Sly."

"I know that you love him. As a matter of fact, everybody knows how much you love him, including him. But, baby girl, love doesn't hurt. Love doesn't abuse, lie, and it damn sure isn't unfaithful. Shit, I'm a smoker, and I'm telling you, there ain't no love in this street game. It's just drugs, money, sex, and lies. I can have sex with anyone or go down on anyone and won't feel nothing for them because I have one motive, and that's my drugs. You know what love is to me?"

"No, what?" I pondered.

Pricy said, "Hugs and kisses."

I repeated, "Hugs and kisses?"

"Yes."

"What's so special about that," I asked.

"Because hugs and kisses show intimacy, which I haven't felt since Money died," she said. "The one thing the streets don't have is intimacy. Hugs and kisses is love, not pussy and munchin'."

Pricy fell in love with this dude named Mark, also known as Money, when she was eighteen and messed with him until she was twenty-six. She loved him. They were like peanut butter and jelly. He got shot and killed while he was hustling. Ever since then, Pricy has been doing her and whoever to support her habit.

"To answer your question about you don't know where to start," Pricy said. "You have to start praying."

"How can I just leave him alone?" I asked. "What about our baby?"

"Twinkle, don't let no dick and everybody's dude cause you to settle for bullshit because he ain't worth it. Stop being so hot in the hips and focus on your life. And if you don't care about your life, think about your children's life. They deserve the best of you and all of you and you need to be whole. I wish I could have some kids, but due to me having so many STDs, my insides are so damaged the doctors told me I will never be able to have children."

Pricy was so good with children. She loved kids, especially little girls; because she loved doing hair and making them look pretty.

"Twinkle, promise me that you will not cheat your kids because Sly cheats you and that you will try your best to get out of this spider web."

"It's too late because I'm already trapped," I said.

"In order to get out of the web, you've got to stop feeding the spider first. Realize that the only reason the spider knows that you are caught is because it senses your struggle by the vibrations transmitted through its web. In knowing this, you must be still and know that God is God because nothing is too hard for him."

Right then, the nurse came in the room and told Pricy it was time for her to leave.

After she left, I kept thinking about what she said. I knew she was telling me the truth. I laid in my bed and cried, wondering how I was going to do this. I have Sly's baby now. I'm officially his baby mom. It's been six years, and Big Boy loves him. How am I going to look if I leave him now?

So many questions were racing through my head. Although I wanted to leave Sly, I couldn't. We are family now. All relationships have problems, but I know Sly loves me. He just gets caught up.

I cried some more, then prayed, "God, I know you to be real. Please help me. I'm in a major mess, and I don't know how to fix it. If Sly is not for me, please remove him peacefully." Then I went to sleep.

Chapter 13

Are You Serious?

"VP, VP, baby, I'm here," Sly whispered and kissed my forehead. It was around seven in the morning.

"What happened to you yesterday?" I asked.

"Babe, I'm sorry, my boys took me to Atlantic City to celebrate baby girl's birth, and they brought me blunts that said it's a girl."

"Why didn't you pick up your phone when I was calling you," I asked.

"I lost my phone."

"Did you find it," I asked.

"No, I never found it. I have to get another one."

"Sly, we are engaged. If you don't think you are going to be faithful to me—to us—then just be honest and let me know. I ask you not to lie and to give me the respect and leave now. I can't afford to allow you to hurt me or our family."

"Babe, I don't want anybody else. I love you and Shaquan and our daughter, and we have longevity. No woman can come close to what we have. I know I should have called and checked on you. I'm sorry, baby. I got caught up. I promise you that I won't do it again."

I wanted to believe Sly so bad, so I made excuses for him. He lost his phone, but he came here first thing in the morning. He apologized with sincerity and promised he wouldn't do it again.

Today was my last day in the hospital. The nurse brought in Anisa. Sly held her while the nurse gave me my discharge instructions.

While he held Anisa, he told her, "Sorry Daddy didn't see you yesterday."

I looked at him like just shut up. *You are always sorry and that's the only area you are consistent in. Being sorry!*

I asked him if he won any money in Atlantic City. Of course he told me no. I knew he didn't go to AC. It was just a matter of time before the truth came out.

My conversations with Diamond and Pricy kept replaying in my mind. Diamond had asked, "Do you think Sly is serious this time? Don't cheat your children because Sly cheats you."

I couldn't believe I was allowing Sly to play me like a desperate broad.

I needed to feed Anisa before we left the hospital. As I looked into her eyes, she stared at me. I felt her spirit talking to me saying, "Mommy, how long are you going to deal with this?"

I answered her back from my spirit, "Don't even worry. Mommy is going to be the best example to you and your brother."

I looked at her and began to see myself. I thought about what happiness, love, and peace truly feels like. I started to feel strong again little by little.

My doctor came in to wish me well. He pinched my cheeks, smiled, and said, "Lisa, don't give up."

177

I was lucky to have a doctor who cared. Many doctors don't take time with patients on state insurance. Not Dr. Hamilton. He really cared about me. During my visits, I told him about the drama with Sly. Dr. Hamilton would always encourage me to never give up.

The doctor left, and it was time to leave the hospital. As I was getting packed, Sly blurted, "Angie, hurry up."

"What did you say, Sly?"

He had this dumb look on his face.

"I asked, who is Angie?" I repeated.

"That's our baby's name," he said.

"No. Even if it was, why would you be calling me her name?"

Sly stuttering, "I don't know. I don't know any Angie."

It's so funny how God will reveal signs and red flags, and we just ignore them. If looks could kill, Sly would have died on demand.

We didn't say anything else to one another until we reached the truck. He had Anisa's car seat put together and in place. As I put the baby in her seat, I heard a vibrating noise from the pouch behind the front passenger seat. It was Sly's phone. I didn't let Sly know that I had "found" it.

When I got into the truck, "If Your Girl Only Knew" by Aliyah was on. I noticed a gold plated hoop earring in the pouch on the side passenger door.

"I guess this is Angie's earring because it damn sure ain't

mine," I said as I showed the earring to Sly.

"That's Dorian's," he said. "I took her food shopping, and she left it."

"When did you take her food shopping?" I asked.

He responded, "Yesterday, and as a matter of fact, she was calling me asking if I saw it."

"Sly, why are you lying? You just told me that you went to AC and that you lost your phone."

"I took her food shopping before I went to AC and before I lost my phone," he said.

"Yeah, whatever."

"I can never win with you," said Sly. "Sometimes I don't know what the use is."

"Because there is no use."

While screaming turn off this damn song. I wanted to tell him about the phone, but I didn't. When we got to my place, I decided to make sure he lost his phone, so I took it as he was carrying my bags inside.

I put Baby Girl in the basinet in my room. I turned on the TV as Sly sat on one couch. I sat on the other.

"Twinkle," he said, breaking the silence. "I'm starting to get real tired of you always accusing me of cheating on you. If you are going to accuse me, then why shouldn't I just do it?"

Why did he go there?

"You and your nugatory reverse psychology can kiss my ass. You cheat, and everybody knows it. You got the game confused because I'm the one who's tired. I'm tired of you cheating on me, and I'm tired of the back and forth. Go home to Angie's because obviously that is who you were with yesterday."

Sly jumped in my face and yelled, "What?"

"Don't let the baby fat fool you," I shouted.

"You know what, I'm out," he said and started for the door.

Without hesitation and with much force I yelled, "Okay, bye."

Sly got back in my face and said, "Bye?"

"Did I stutter? Yes, bye," I repeated. "What? You deaf now?"

"You fat bitch," he said. "You ain't shit."

"Sly, I don't care if I was four hundred pounds; I will always be the shit! You hear me, Sly? The shit! Unlike your tall, looking-like-Jay Jay, toilet-bowl, pilgarlic, old ass. Get the f@#$% out my face. I make you look good. Never forget that. I make you relevant because you are here in Jersey. I'm the reason why your boys big you up. Because they all want me! Four hundred pounds and all! They can't figure out why am I with an ugly-ass, broke, old man. So don't forget I am the shit!"

Sly spit in my face and shouted, "F@#$%you, bitch." He damn near ran out my apartment.

I wiped my face off and ran to the door and yelled, "Dummy! I know where you live, and I promise you I'm coming for you!"

I slammed the door.

"This lunatic done messed up for real," I screamed out loud.

My parents would be picking Big Boy up from day camp around five in the afternoon, so I had time to wind down and get my mind right before he came home.

I called Kay to tell her what happened.

"How much is it going to take for you to get it? Sly never is going to change. Me and everyone else knows that, but you have to get it. That six-carat rock is not worth your life. Shaquan and Anisa are worth your life and more, but you need to get the memo because Sly is never going to leave you."

"You don't think so," I asked.

"Hey, valley girl, take off the blonde wig. Why in hell would he leave you? You are his safe haven, a good girl that works, lives in Jersey, takes good care of her kids, and, furthermore, you genuinely love him. He knows that, and he knows that you are not going to cheat on him. Hell, we all know that, but what I can't figure out is why won't you cheat on him."

"Because I really love him," I said.

"I wished he loved you the same way," she said.

Just then Anisa woke up. I told Kay that we'd talk later.

Before we hung up, she said, "Twinkle, the only thing Sly loves doing is using you. His love will always hurt you because he doesn't care about himself. Girl, I have some more knives, gloves, and a plastic bag if you want to do road kill rodent part two."

We laughed.

I confessed, "Girl, I'm going to get revenge, trust me. I haven't figured it out yet, but you definitely will hear about it."

"I know I will because you have an imagination for dat ass."

We laughed some more and hung up.

I picked up Anisa. "Everything is going to be all right," I told her. I know what I had to do, but I didn't want to do it because leaving Sly would be hard. It's easy to leave somebody alone when you're mad, but it's not that easy when you're no longer mad.

I fed baby girl, and she eventually went back to sleep. My parents arrived with Big Boy. He was so excited to see his baby sister he couldn't stop kissing her and telling her how much he loved her.

I wanted them to be close and to have a brother-and-sister bond. So I let him hold her whenever he asked, and he asked often.

A couple days later, Pricy called. I told her about the beef with Sly. She asked when I was going back to work. I told her in about two months and asked why she wanted to know.

"Twinkle, I'm trying to kick this habit, and I need something else to do."

"Well, you are always welcome to stay with me," I told her. "As a matter of fact, you can come through tonight or tomorrow. I still have to get Sly back for spitting in my face. I need to find out who this Angie chick is."

"Twinkle, how long is the tit for tat going to go on?"

"I don't know, and I don't care, nobody is going to spit in

my face and get away with it."

"Okay, Twinkle, do you."

"When are you coming over?" I asked.

"I'll try to have one of my old, rich men bring me over tonight," Pricy replied.

I was glad that Pricy was coming through because I could sleep or run errands while she stayed with the kids. Plus, she didn't mind cleaning and cooking. And her decorating skills were up. She could decorate and paint your house and, I promise you, your house would be looking like it should be in someone's magazine. And she would keep my weaves up – all for free.

She was always a good help, and the bonus was she loved me. Pricy was gifted, but that monkey she was dealing with was very real.

Pricy arrived the next morning before I took Big Boy to day camp. I was glad she came when she did because that meant I didn't have to get Baby Girl dressed. I explained to Big Boy that cousin Pricy was going to be staying with us for a while. I told him that she needs a friend because she is trying to get over a drug problem, but she would never harm him or his sister. However, if he ever felt uncomfortable around her or saw something that he never saw before, all he needed to do was to let me know.

Now that Shaquan was older, I liked to be upfront with him. There is no future in frontin' with your children because the fact of the matter is they already know. Anyway, I loved Pricy, but I wasn't stupid and I loved my kids more.

"I really like cousin Pricy because she acts just like me," Shaquan smiled.

I asked him what he meant.

"She acts like a kid, and she is funny."

"Cousin Pricy is funny in more ways than you would understand," I told him.

I dropped him off at day camp and returned home. I told Pricy that I was going to Philly.

"What are you going to do?" she asked.

My plan was to pour a bottle of bleach on his truck. Then pour thirty-six cracked eggs, in a container, and have his truck look mottled.

"If you're going to do it, do it at night so the eggs can be dry and crusty in the morning," she said.

Being that it is hot, the eggs will fry right on his truck and the bleach will discolor the paint.

"That's right," I told Pricy. "He spit on my face, and I'm going to spit on his truck."

"Twinkle, you always had a bad temper," Pricy said. "When you were younger, I knew you were going to have a bad temper."

"How?" I asked.

"Because your nose would always sweat. People whose nose sweats always have a bad temper," she explained.

"Pricy, you and your old wives' tales."

"It is truth in that, and that's how I have survived the streets this long," she added. "Shaquan's nose sweats too."

"I hope his temper ain't like mine," I said.

"Well, you better start praying so God can calm that thing down," she said.

"Okay. But I'm driving to Philly now just to see if I'm going to see him."

Pricy responded, "Okay."

I told her that Anisa's milk was prepared, and I would see her in a few.

It was around 1:30 p.m., and I was on the road to Philly. When I pulled up, Ms. Bonnie was sitting on the porch, so I went over to talk with her.

"You had the baby," she asked.

"Yes. I named her Anisa Queen Dior Valentine. She was a big baby, nine pounds and some change," I said proudly.

Ms. Bonnie said, "What!"

"Yeah. My cousin is watching her now. I decided to drive out here to get out the apartment and to get some fresh air," I paused. "Ms. Bonnie, have you seen Sly?"

"I just don't know what you see in him because, like I told you before, you are better off without him," she said. "I saw him walking with Na'tif."

I asked, "Who is Na'tif?"

"Her real name is Angie," Ms. Bonnie said.

Ah! The woman who left the earring in Sly's truck, I thought.

"Why do they call her Na' tif," I asked.

"It stands for no toes and no fingers," she answered.

"What," I yelled in disbelief.

Ms. Bonnie continued. "She was born that way because her mom is a heavy drug user and so is she."

"Why would Sly be messing with her," I wondered out loud.

Ms. Bonnie had the answer.

"They say she give head like no other," she pointed out.

"Ms. Bonnie, I can't believe you said that."

She wasn't moved by my shocked reaction and kept right on talking.

"Twinkle that is all these young boys be talking about. She's not really bad-looking. She just has those deformities."

"She's a crackhead with no toes and fingers. First, Buf, now this chick," I said. "Wow, Sly knows how to pick them."

"I've known Sly since he's been a little boy. He used to mess with my niece when they were fifteen, and he had a lot of women then. He never had a preference," Ms. Bonnie said. "Sly will mess with anybody, and I do mean anybody. He just lucked out with you. Twinkle, Sly is not the man for you."

My mind was working. "Where does this Angie girl live?"

"In those apartments on Lame Street. She has six kids, and she let them do whatever they want," Ms. Bonnie said. "Twinkle, stop letting your mistakes be your losses and make your mistakes become your victory."

"How am I going to do that?" I asked.

"It's so simple. Learn from your mistakes," she said. "When am I going to see the baby?"

I told her I would probably bring her out in few weeks. Ms. Bonnie told me to be sure to stop by because she was going to get her some diapers.

"Thank you, Ms. Bonnie. I will talk to you later."

I got in my car and drove to Lame Street. I didn't see Sly's truck, so I went home because I was a little nervous that Pricy was with Baby Girl.

My apartment was spotless, and baby girl was chilling.

"Pricy, I don't mind you staying here, but one thing I ask is for you not to steal from me or get high in here. If you do, I will call the police on you and make sure you get locked up for a long time. Please don't play me."

"I will never disrespect you or your house," Pricy promised. "You already know how I do. When I get high, nobody will be able to find me. The day I want to get high, I will leave."

"Talking about you leaving and nobody being able to find you," I said, "when you get high, where do you go?"

"All you need to know is that I be around."

"Around where, Pricy?"

"I will never tell you because you don't need to be there looking for me. There are some things you don't need to know because if you look for trouble, you will find it. And you might find somebody there you know that you wasn't looking for."

Pricy was keeping something from me. We didn't say anything for a few minutes, and then Pricy quickly said, "I have two hundred dollars on my food stamp card. You can use it anytime you want."

"What you trying to say, Pricy? I don't have enough food in here?"

"That's what I was thinking, but you just said it."

"Let me get the card so we can get our grub on," I told her.

She told me to get the food, and she would cook it because she has to keep busy.

"You ain't said nothing but a word."

"Your closet is a mess," Pricy said. "The only closet that is together is Shaquan's."

"I know. Sly cleaned it out and told him that he had to keep it together," I told her.

"Talking about Sly, did you see him?" she asked.

"No. I didn't see his truck either, but I found out who he is messing with and where she lives."

"Who is she?" Pricy asked.

"This girl named Angie," I said, "but they call her Na'tif."

Pricy repeated the name as if she knew her, so I asked if she did.

"Everybody in the tri-state area knows no toes and fingers," said Pricy.

"Well, I don't," I answered.

"I know my peoples just like musicians know musicians,

hair dressers know hair dressers, and crackheads know crackheads," she said. "But just for the simple fact that she don't have no toes and fingers she stands out even the more. They say munchin' is her gift."

"Ms. Bonnie told me the same thing. Wow! What she be doing—sucking the blood out of it? I will never understand that lifestyle," I said. "And I don't know how I even got caught up with it."

"I can tell you how you got caught up in it," Pricy said. "By messin' with Sly's crackhead ass. He let his old tricks become his same trick when you his, new trick, leaves."

"What, Pricy?"

"Sly gets high, but when he is with you, he doesn't because he knows you don't play that. So he is temporarily clean and in touch with reality when he is with you, but as soon as he crosses that bridge, he is doing things you wouldn't even imagine. You are considered Sly's new trick. He knows whatever he does to you. You will always take him back because he knows he is your habit. So therefore, you are his new trick. Break your habit, and then you will break free."

I told Pricy that I would break the habit! After I bleach and egg his truck tonight! Nobody is going to spit in my face and get away with it!

"One day, you are going to grow up and out of Sly," she said.

"I believe you," I admitted. "But before that day comes, Sly

189

and everybody else is going to know whose boss."

"I hear that," Pricy said.

She gave me the card, and I went food shopping. While I was out, I picked up Big Boy from camp. He spent the entire ride back home telling me how much fun he had and how he passed the deep water test and can swim in six feet now. He said he loved to swim. He was so hyped, and I was hyped for him.

When we got home, Big Boy gave his sister a kiss and told her that he missed her.

We had a relaxed evening while Pricy cooked dinner, but as the night went on, I started feeling angry that Sly had not called to check on us. I guess he planned the argument perfectly because he knew that we couldn't have sex until six weeks later. That bastard! Now he is messing with no toes, no fingers, all the hoes, and next will be monopodes. Around ten in the evening, I told Pricy I would be back. She already knew what I was going to do. I drove to Philly again. Sly's truck wasn't outside his apartment. I drove by that girl Na'tif's apartment. Still no truck. So I went past the "Bumpy Road" bar. Bingo!

I parked and got my two big containers of bleach and egg mixture. I didn't care about the people standing outside bustin' it up. As I started to pour the bleach on the truck, I heard someone say, "Oh shit! Is that Twinkle?"

"Yeah it's me," I hollered. As I poured the egg mixture on his truck.

Sly ran out the bar.

"Bitch !" he yelled.

"Bitch what," I said.

As he approached me, I planned to throw bleach in his eyes. He got close and was ready to hit me when Candi's brother, Michael, appeared out of nowhere.

"I'm not going to let you hit Twinkle," he said as he stood in between Sly and me.

Sly was about to hit him, but Candi's brother beat him to the punch by hitting him over the head with his Heineken bottle. Blood was everywhere.

Some guys ran over and grabbed Michael. Others grabbed Sly.

Someone shouted, "Twinkle, go home!"

I walked to my car and drove clean off. In the rearview mirror, I saw Sly get into his truck. I thought he might follow me. If he planned to, he changed his mind.

When I got home, Pricy was waiting.

"What happened?" she asked.

I told her everything.

"You know that I was praying for you," Pricy said.

"Why?"

"Twinkle, you just had a baby, you have stitches, your body just been freshly wounded, and you in Philly acting a fool," she said. "You didn't even give your body a chance to heal. I asked God to intervene on your behalf and to send an angel of protection to protect your crazy ass."

"Well, God heard, and he answered because Michael came out of nowhere and told Sly that he was not going to do nothing to me," I said. "Child, he conked him clear over the head with his Heineken bottle."

"I hope he knocked some good sense into him," Pricy said.

I started singing that throwback song, "Oops, upside your head. I said oops, upside your head by the Gap Band lead singer Charlie Wilson."

Pricy chimed in, "What! What! I said oops, upside your head. I said oops, upside your head. Now together…"

I joined her, "I said, oops upside your head. I said oops, upside your head."

We cracked up.

Then Pricy said, "Twinkle, I have to step out for a minute."

"Okay, but don't come back if you on," I told her.

"I will be back in a few days."

"Okay, and I want you to know that I will be praying for you." I added. "We are both going to stop all of our bad habits."

We hugged. I told her that I loved her and that I will see her in a few days.

Shortly after Pricy left, my phone rang. It was Sly. I answered, "Hey, Mike I was being smart."

"Twinkle, this has gone too far," he murmured.

"It wasn't too far when you spit in my face. It wasn't too far when you didn't come to the hospital. It wasn't too far when I saw your phone in the back pouch of your truck. Oh yeah, before you tell me another lie, I threw your phone out after I found it.

The only reason why it's too far is because now I have retaliated. I will continue to retaliate if you keep disrespecting me."

"Twinkle, listen," said Sly. "I'm in the hospital now, and I have to get a tetanus shot, and stitches."

"So? What do you want me to do, come to the hospital, Sly? Not!"

Then I banged on him. He called back.

"I want all of this to be over."

"It is over," I screamed. "It's been over, so leave me alone."

"I don't want you," he roared. "It's all about my daughter."

"Well, let's keep it that way and do this for your daughter, keep it moving. Regardless, we are good. You are the one in the hospital whining and calling me, getting stitched up. Oh by the way, don't go to sleep."

I banged on him again and took a shower. I tried to get some sleep. Being that I'm breastfeeding, I was up for it seemed like every two hours with Anisa. Boy, did I miss my sleep.

Chapter 14
Sucker

I was so tired in the morning that I told Shaquan that I wasn't taking him to camp. We were going to relax. Big Boy was cool because he wanted to chill.

"Mommy, where is Sly?" he asked.

"I guess home," I lied to my son. "Why do you ask?"

"I had a bad dream about him last night."

"What was it about?"

"I had a dream that someone shot him, and he died. Mom, it was so real."

"Baby, Sly is fine," I tried to console him.

"Can I call him to say hi to him?" Shaquan asked.

I acted as if I didn't hear him.

"Mom," he said in an elevated tone, "can I call Sly?"

"Yes, you can call him, but let's just call him later."

"Mommy, I don't want to call him later. I want to call him now."

"Little boy, who you think you talkin' to?"

"Mommy, I just want to make sure that he is okay."

I said okay, but I really didn't want Shaquan calling Sly because of what just happened. I didn't want Sly to think that I put him up to calling him. But Big Boy was persistent just like me.

I acted like I was dialing Sly's number and told Shaquan

that he didn't answer. Shaquan urged me to try again. I looked at this little boy like he needs to go ahead somewhere.

"Can you write down the number for me?" Shaquan asked. "I will call him myself."

Shaquan was too darn smart for his own good. I wrote Sly's number on a piece of paper. He really loved Sly. He was the only man around since Shaquan was ten months old, and he had a special bond with Sly. I believe Sly loved him too.

Shaquan dialed his number. I heard him say, "What's up, man?"

I looked at Big Boy, like, okay.

Then I heard him say, "Shaquan," then he smiled.

I don't know what Sly said, but Shaquan asked when was he coming over so he can beat him in a game of chess.

"Okay." He paused. "Mom, Sly wants to talk to you."

"Hello," I said with an attitude.

"You know my truck looks like a Dalmatian," Sly said.

"Too bad."

"How's my daughter doing?"

"Great. How do you really think that she is doing?" I asked sarcastically. "You ain't here taking care of her."

"Why did you have Shaquan call me," Sly asked.

"I didn't have him call you. He wanted to call you because he had a bad dream about you."

Shaquan was in his room watching TV, and I was in my bedroom.

I told Sly how I ignored Big Boy when he asked to call him, but he asked if I would give him the number so he could call himself.

"I promised him that I will be over soon to play a game of chess with him. And I want to see my daughter."

"Sly, you can come over. I really don't care one way or the other."

"Twinkle, where is all the hostility coming from?"

"Sly, I'm not even going to get myself upset because I didn't want to talk to you no way. I'm hanging up," I said and then banged on him.

I walked out my room, and Big Boy was standing there.

"Is Sly coming over?" he asked.

"Not today," I answered.

"I hope it's soon because I will be starting first grade soon."

"I know when you will be starting first grade," I chuckled. "But what does first grade have to do with anything?"

"Because I will have real homework."

"You're right," I told him. "And you will have to study hard."

"Thanks, Mom, for letting me call Sly. I'm glad he is okay."

"I told you he was," I grinned.

We hugged.

"Where is Cousin Pricy," he asked.

"Boy, you got too much time on your hands. You should have went to camp," I told him. "But she will be back soon. When Cousin Pricy is here, do you wish she was here or do you wish that she wasn't here?"

"I love when she is here because she fixes me brownies."

"Boy, you love to eat just like your mom. Yeah, those brownies she made the other day were bangin'. Between Cousin Pricy and Sly, I don't know who's going to make us fatter."

"Mom, I'm not going to be fat, I'm going to have muscles."

"Excuse me. You go ahead and get those muscles."

A week and a half passed before Sly mustered the nerve to call.

I picked up and said, "What's good?"

"You and my kids."

"Whatever, Sly. What do you want?"

"I still see that you are on some husky shit."

"Yep," I said. "I'm going to stay on my mano a mano because I finally realized that you can't make chicken salad out of chicken shit. You need chicken."

"Twinkle, you need to go to the doctors because I think you have that depression shit, that thing that women get after they have a baby."

"Sly, are you serious? Now you are trying to diagnose me with post-partum depression," I said. "No, you moron, I don't have post-partum depression. I have post-Sly ass. I can't stand you, and leave me alone."

I felt like I hated Sly. It seemed like everything that he did to me kept replaying in my mind, and I was beginning to see the truth. I wasn't feeling him at all. The thought of him made me sick.

A wise man once told me that love is the most sacred place. When it is injured, the soul seeks to protect it, and the devil initiates hate to be the protecting shield.

I hated Sly, and I didn't care if I ever saw or talked to him again. I wanted him out of my life completely.

"Can I come over to see Shaquan and my daughter?" Sly asked.

"Only if you give me some bread."

He asked, "How much do you need?"

"At least a G."

He repeated what I said as if he didn't understand.

"A ..., G? What do you need a thousand dollars for?" he asked.

"Either you're going to have it or you won't be seeing your daughter," I told him.

"Twinkle, I just got my truck repainted."

"Ummm, I don't care. Remember, you spit in my face."

"Is this what this is about?" Sly said.

"It's about everything," I answered, "everything from 1994 up 'til now."

Sly said he would have the money next week so he could come over then. He also wanted to take Shaquan shopping for school.

"Yeah, aight," I said and hung up.

Sly called me back. "What!"

He asked, "Twinkle, you really hate me."

"You damn right."

"I never loved a woman the way I love you," Sly replied.

"Sly, I heard it all before. Tell me something I don't know. Like who you smashing and who is marking your neck all up."

"All right, Twinkle, I'll talk to you later."

After we hung up, I tended to Big Boy and Anisa, cleaned the house, cooked dinner, and relaxed.

In the meantime, Labor Day was coming up, and Sly called a couple days before the holiday. He told me he had the money and wanted to take Shaquan school shopping. I asked if he had my grand. He said he did.

"Well, come through," I told him.

It was around ten in the morning on Saturday, and Shaquan was so excited, but of course, I wasn't. Sly had told Shaquan that he was going to buy him some school clothes and that he was going to get some things for his sister.

Baby Girl had everything. Between my family and friends, she was good. Although I didn't have a baby shower, my family was very supportive, Sly's family was not. They were only halfway supportive when Sly and me were cool. They were sometimey just like him. Everything is everybody's fault besides their own, and they never want to be accountable for their own actions. Watch who you have a baby by because the apple does not fall too far from the tree.

When Sly got to my apartment, he went straight to the refrigerator.

"You got a whole lot of food in here."

"I know."

"Why so much?" he asked.

Before I could say anything, Big Boy said, "Because sometimes cousin Pricy comes over and watches me and my sister."

Sly gave me a look like, "Why is she here?" He knew that Pricy was a smoker. I was waiting for him to say something about her. I wanted him to say something so bad so I could go on him. All nine of his baby moms are smokers, and he was fine with them watching his babies. Ooh! I was waiting, but he must have felt my vibe because he changed the subject.

"Shaquan," he said, "do you want to go out?"

He answered, "Yeah, man!"

"I want to take you to Fifth Street and buy you some underwear, undershirts, socks, a few jeans, and some shirts. And if you're good," Sly said, "I'm going to buy you some sneakers. While we are out, we will get some grub."

Sly held Baby Girl for a few. He kissed and talked to her, saying who knows what. Frankly, I didn't even care. Around 12:45 p.m., we all were getting ready to leave, but I decided that I didn't want to go.

"Sly, you and Shaquan can go without me. I'll stay home with Baby Girl because I don't want to take her out."

It was as if what I said didn't faze Sly.

"Oh yeah, I almost forgot to tell you, Ms. Bonnie bought our daughter some Pampers. I have them in my truck."

"Aww! That was so nice. She kept her word," I said. "Okay, just give them to me when you and Shaquan come back."

Shaquan was so souped he was hanging out with Sly that I could feel his anticipation. Before they left, I asked Sly for my money. He gave me $500.

"I didn't ask for $500. You are short."

"I know, VP. Something came up, plus I'm taking Shaquan shopping."

"Whatever," I said.

I gave Big Boy a hug and kiss and told him to have fun. Then Sly went to kiss me, and I pulled away. He looked so hurt.

"See you later, Twinkle."

"As soon as they left, I got baby girl together and went to the bank. I knew he would ask for it back if I kept dissin' him so I didn't want the money in the apartment."

It was so relaxing to be home with just me and Baby Girl. She was just like me—she loved to sleep and eat, and she wasn't a cry baby at all. As a matter of fact, Big Boy wasn't a cry baby either.

While Sly and Shaquan were gone, I joined Baby Girl in our favorite activities. We acted like bears, and we ate and slept.

The doorbell rang around 6:30 p.m. I was greeted by Big Boy's big smile when I opened the door. He had two big bags of clothes in each hand. He couldn't wait to show me.

"Mom, Sly got me a pair of Jordans," he said as he came inside.

"That is so nice."

Sly bought you back some Popeye's chicken and biscuits. That was a good look because I was starting to get hungry again.

Big Boy showed me all of his new clothes.

"Everything I wanted, Sly got for me," Shaquan said.

"Because you deserve it," I replied.

"Let's put your clothes away," Sly said.

I guess Sly was organizing his drawers and closets again for his new clothes. After they were finished, he showed me the outfits he bought Anisa. They were so cute. That's one thing I couldn't take away from Sly—he had a keen eye for fashion.

"VP, I want to have a Labor Day cookout tomorrow for you and the kids. I want to grill some hot dogs, hamburgers, and shrimp and make some potato and shrimp salad, along with some corn on the cob, with some watermelon and fruit salad. I just wanna relax."

"So what you saying? You want to stay the night?" I asked.

"Yeah, I want to chill with my family."

"Okay, but when Anisa gets up in the middle of the night, you have to get up to change and feed her."

He was cool with that.

As the evening went on, Shaquan and Sly played chess, and he started teaching him how to play spades. Around ten in the evening, he ordered pizza, and he started boiling the potatoes for the cookout.

Shaquan started getting sleepy around 11:30 p.m. I put him to bed. Baby girl was already sleeping. Sly and I watched TV, but we didn't speak much.

Around one in the morning, I took a shower. Sly came in the bathroom and stood by the shower curtain.

"Twinkle, I miss you."

"Sly, tonight is not the night. I'm not in the mood."

He said okay and went back into the living room.

When I got out of the shower, I put my grandma PJs on and went to bed.

Then I felt Sly kissing me on my cheek and neck. I acted like I was still sleep. He kept it up for what seemed like fifteen minutes. Then I felt his hand touching me down below like he was a pianist.

"Sly, we ain't doing this," I snapped.

"VP, don't you miss me?" he whined.

"No, not really," I answered.

"You don't miss how good I make you feel?" He asked.

I sat up because I had to get my attitude straight for this response.

"The mouth you kiss me with is the same mouth you used to spit in my face. The hands you caress me with are the same hands that you held your pistol to my head. And you're so called trophy that used to make me feel so good makes a whole lot of others feel good too. That's why you always burning. So, no, I don't miss you." Saying in my Kool Moe Dee tone, I yelled. "Go see the doctor."

"Baby," he was whispering. "Let me make it up to you."

"How are you going to do that, Sly? By getting me pregnant again? Leave me alone because I'm tired and you're not getting any. So you can whack off. I don't care, just leave me alone."

Saying no felt so empowering. That moment, I decided to make the word *no* a major part of my vocabulary from here on out because all the word *yes* did was stress me the hell out. That night, I realized the power of the word *no*.

Did you ever notice when a child is like two or three, whatever you ask them they are always saying no. You know why? It is because that is the time they figure out they have a voice and they feel like they don't have to listen because they are coming into their own person. That's how I felt. All the control that I had lost was now back in full force. People only do what you allow them to do to you.

"Can I hold you?" Sly asked.

"Yes, as long as I don't feel your dick poking me in my back."

"Just forget it," he said in frustration.

I went to sleep and slept good. I heard Anisa wake up a few

times, and Sly changed, fed, and burped her. I didn't move.

He woke up early and fixed breakfast—pancakes and sausages. I really wasn't that hungry, but I ate a little.

Sly and Shaquan did a lot of talking. Eventually, he had Big Boy help him peel the potatoes. Baby girl and I chilled.

I maybe said two words to Sly. Around 12:30 p.m., he cleaned the grill and the chicken. I didn't know that he went to the supermarket early morning to get everything he needed for the cookout. Until Shaquan told me when he asked could he eat his Slim Jim.

Chapter 15
The Gathering

Sly bought enough food to feed the whole town, so I called my sis and my home girls and told them that we are having a Labor Day cookout. I told them to come over around four in the afternoon for some good food and drinks. Everybody knew that Sly could cook.

My sis brought a big bottle of 1738 and her friend Isaiah. They been messing with each other on and off for about three and half years. Isaiah was cool. I believed he really loved my sis, but she had commitment issues and wasn't ready to settle. But when he was around, she was content. Isaiah was a gentleman and had plenty of dough. I thought he was good for her because she didn't have any kids, nor did he.

Kay arrived next with her friend GQ and her son, JT. She had a different friend for every occasion. That was just Kay. She bought over her special sushi rolls, and them little things is good.

Bertha came over with her longtime boyfriend, Michael. He is Jamaican, and he is cool peeps. He paid for Bertha and me to go to Jamaica one year, and we had a blast. Michael was like a brother to me for real. He always came with that Jamaican dro. Nothing in America was messing with that. Michael loved the ground Bertha walked on and was a good father to their son Antwain. He had a very good heart. They came with some curry chicken and rice.

Michael had taught Bertha how to make some Jamaican dishes, and he taught her well.

C and Ree with their crazy boyfriends were the last to arrive. Their boyfriends were cut from the same cloth Sly was cut from—sickening.

C came over with a big jug of spring water. She always wanted to do what was right. On the other hand, her man, T-Bone, was straight local. They had been together just as long as Sly and I had been together. He was mentally and physically abusive to C for no reason. I couldn't stand him. We would always argue, and we almost fought once, but C calmed him down. C was my sweetest friend, and she had a personality that she could get along with anybody. Sometimes, she was too nice. They had one son named Joshua, and he was smart as a whip.

Ree came with her famous deviled eggs and pasta salad, her totally off boyfriend, Nap, was with her. Word on the street is he got the name because he had a reputation for knocking cats out in fights. They said when he knocked someone out; it looked like they were taking a nap. Nite - nite. Nap had that name every since I've known him, and that's been years. We all were chilling while Mad Lion "Take It Easy" was playing.

So everyone had arrived except Pricy. The boys were in Shaquan's room playing games, and Anisa was in my room sleeping. The men were outside talking, smoking, and drinking while Sly was grilling. The ladies were sipping, talking, laughing, and listening to music. It was an intimate, relaxing day with friends and family.

Out of nowhere, Kay tells me, "You look happy."

"Yeah, I'm happy because I finally pushed Anisa out."

Diamond said, "Yeah, I know, sis. It looks like you dropped like one hundred pounds already because I don't see the double chin."

"Sis, don't start," I said.

Everyone laughed.

"When are you and Sly planning to get married?" C asked.

Before I could answer, Bertha said, "C, please you need to see and catch the ball. They are not getting married."

Then Ree intervened. "I know that would make you very happy, Twinkle."

"Ladies, real talk," I admitted. "I'm not even feeling him like that anymore."

"Thank God," Kay said loudly.

"Hey, Twinkle." It was Diamond. "Have you started putting that stuff on you and Anisa's forehead?"

"Yes, my baby girl frown mark is going away."

Then C asked if I've been praying.

I responded yes.

"God does answer prayer," said Kay, "because I've been praying that you would leave Sly alone for good."

"Twinkle, are you sure you don't want to be with him?" said Ree. "I mean, you are now officially family."

"Ree, do you really want to be with Nap?" I asked. "And

let's keep it real."

"No," she answered. "But I've been with him all these years, and I really don't know how to start over again."

"That's how I feel," C said. "Now, since we have a son together, oftentimes I wonder if another man is going to really want to be with me."

"It shouldn't matter how many kids you have," I said. "You can have four, five, six kids. When a man truly loves you, he will love you and your children."

"Y'all need to experience real love," Bertha said.

"What is real love because love has no guarantees," Diamond said.

"Yeah, it's not guaranteed, but one thing I do know is that real love does not abuse you. All of y'all have these men that is physically, mentally, and emotionally abusive, and y'all stay. For the life of me, I can't understand why y'all stay. Is it because they make you climax? If that's the reason, you can find someone else to make you climax and love you at the same time. Now that's what I call having your ice cream and cake."

"Bertha," I said. "You just lucked up with a nice guy so you can't understand what the rest of us are going through."

Kay chimed in, "Bertha, all men can't make you climax. As a matter of fact, most of them come too fast and they don't even give you an opportunity to participate."

"That's why I keeps it pimpin'," Diamond said.

We all laughed.

I told the girls, "The reality of knowing that my relationship with Sly isn't going to last really hurts because all the years I invested were basically wasted. I feel like he robbed me of my youth. The hurt feels like someone shot me in my heart, and now I have a hole in it. I feel empty inside. At the same time, I feel like my insides are being torn apart. It feels as if my soul is connected to him like an umbilical cord, and every time I try to move on, the pain reminds me of the love I once had for him. This tug of war inside of me is the ripping and tearing from me trying to detach. I don't know which pain hurts the most—him cheating and lying or this pain of trying to detach from him. This sexual ungodly soul tie has me caught in a dysfunctional cycle. Lauryn Hill, kept it all the way one hundred with her song "Ex- Factor" because that's how I'm feeling. Every night I ask God to help me break free, but it doesn't seem like he hears me."

"He hears you," said Diamond. "But God is not an abracadabra God. So many of us think that we can ask God to do something, and then *pow*! It's done. God is not a magician, but God will not let you go through without bringing you out and bettering you. And that's free, sis."

Sly walked in and said, "The food is ready. Y'all can eat."

As my girls went outside, Sly asked if he could talk to me in my bedroom. By now, that "devil oil" was inside of him. We walked into the room.

"What's up?" I asked him.

"I miss you, and I need to have you tonight."

"Why?" I asked.

He tried to kiss me, but I backed up.

"Baby, you are so damn sexy, and I want you."

"Sly, leave me alone," I said apathetically while walking out the room.

Sly had an attitude, but of course, I didn't care.

Everyone got their grub on. I fed Baby Girl and changed her. Around 8:30 p.m., C poured herself some more wine. As she walked back to the sofa, she accidently tripped and spilled some wine on T-Bone's shirt.

"You clumsy bitch," he yelled at her. To everyone else, he said, "C must be getting tired because she always gets clumsy when she gets tired."

She was mentally tired more than anything else. I said, "T-Bone, you need to calm the hell down."

Frantically, C said, "Baby, I'm sorry," as she wiped the wine off his shirt.

T-Bone glared at me and said, "Twinkle, mind your business."

"Man, it ain't that deep. We just chillin' with our ladies," Sly said, a poor attempt to lighten the situation.

T-Bone told C they were leaving and called Joshua. I didn't like how he grabbed C's arm. I was so angry I followed them outside.

"You are not going to be disrespecting my house, you punk ass," I yelled.

Diamond came out and said, "Sis, fall back. This is not your fight."

I wanted to fight him so bad. We walked back inside. The atmosphere was off—like T-Bone started a chain reaction.

Nap started on Ree.

"Why do you keep getting up and getting something to eat?"

"Because this is a BBQ," Ree said.

"You just keep getting up so everybody can look at your high ass," Nap hollered. "I told you not to wear those tight jeans anyway."

"Nap, I'm not C, and you need to shut the hell up and eat because you are drunk and high," Ree said.

"I will leave your ass here, Ree," said Nap.

"I don't care, because I'm done with you anyway."

Oh shit! It's on.

Ree and I were alike; we were not scared of our crazy men. We would fight them in a minute without a care of who's around.

Then Diamond started with the jokes.

"This is what I get for bringing that big bottle of 1738," she said. "Sorry, everybody."

Diamond's man said, "Yep, it's time for us to go."

Everybody agreed.

I asked everyone to make a plate to take home first. Plates were made, good-byes were said, and Diamond volunteered to watch Shaquan again.

"I don't want ole boy trying to stay the night."

"What is it?" I said. "There must be a full moon tonight causing us to be tired of our men."

Diamond said, "It's that time of the month and I don't feel like entertaining any company."

So I got Big Boy's bags ready. He was always excited to go over his aunt's apartment.

Once everybody was gone, Sly and I sat on the sofa together.

"What's up with your friends?" he asked.

I said, "They're crazy just like you. Hey, thanks for the cookout. Despite of the drama, I still had a good time with my girls."

"No problem, baby," said Sly, and he kissed me. "Are you going to help me clean?"

I told him my plans included showering and going to bed and nothing else.

I hurried in the shower because I knew Sly was going to try to get a peeky peek. He came in right as I turned the water off and startled me.

"Sly, can I dry myself off?"

"Let me do it."

"No, Sly. I'm good."

Sly said in disgust, "Who is he?"

I repeated, "Who is he?" Then, puzzled, I asked, "Who's he?"

"The dude's balls that is touching your ass," he said.
I laughed. "Are you serious? What you think, I'm doing it doggy style with someone else?" I laughed some more, then walked out the bathroom into my room, while shaking my head. Sly followed me.

"Are you going to argue with me in front of Anisa while she is asleep?" I said.

"Nah, but after you get dressed, come into the living room."

So Sly left the room, and I started praying for God to help me because I didn't want to argue. All I wanted to do was sleep. As I walked into the living room, I said, "Baby, I don't want to argue."

"Well, don't," Sly barked.

I sat down next to him.

"VP, just be real with me and tell me if you're messing with another dude."

"That's how you really feel about me? You think that because I'm not making love to you I have to be doing somebody else?"

"You never told me no before," Sly responded.

"Did it ever cross your mind that I might get tired of you cheating on me?" I asked.

"VP," he said quickly, "you cheat too."

"If you think that, why do you want to sleep with me? Then I started to walk away."

But Sly jumped up and grabbed me.

"Because you belong to me and I invested a lot of time in this pussy."

"Oh, I'm an investment, Sly? Well, you got your dividends because Anisa is here. So now, there is no need for us."

Sly pushed me against the wall. "Twinkle, I'm going to hurt you. Now act like you know and give me what belongs to me."

"Have you lost it?" I yelled at him. "This is my pussy, and you better go ahead somewhere."

As I walked away, Sly hollered, "I'm going to kill you tonight, and I'm going to call the cops to let them know there is about to be a murder."

He picked up the house phone and dialed 911. He told the dispatcher he was about to commit a murder and they needed to come now. I ran in my room, grabbed my Mace, ran back into the living room, and sprayed him.

Sly dropped to his knees and yelled, "Twinkle, I'm sorry. I was only playing with you."

I yelled back, "That's your damn problem! You think life is a game, and that's why you live so frivolously. But my life means everything to me. I'm not going to allow you or anyone else to take it away from me or strip it from me. I'm done with you!"

Before you knew it, the police were at the door. I let them in, and they rushed over to Sly, cuffed him, and escorted him out of my apartment.

One of the officers asked me to come to the police station for some questioning. I got Anisa and drove to the police station.

When I arrived, Sly was in a holding cell. I was directed to a room where I was interviewed. I told the officers I didn't want to press chargers but did request a restraining order. The officer informed me that even though I didn't press charges, the state would because his threat is considered terroristic.

About an hour after I returned home, Sly called. He was crying. "Twinkle, the judge let me out on an own recognizance."

"What do you want me to do?" I asked.

"They drove me to a hotel here in Jersey, but I can't get my truck being that you have a restraining order against me."

"You damn right. You threatened to murder me, and not only that, you took it to another level and called the cops. You are losing it, Sly! I don't know what's going on with you upstairs, but I don't trust how you are moving."

"Baby, I will never hurt you," he sobbed.

"But I will hurt you because you bring out the worse in me, Sly." I wasn't even trying to be smart; I was being so serious.

"Twinkle, I need my truck."

"Well, come and get it because I don't want it," I told him.

He asked how was he going to get it, and I told him he should have thought about that before he called the cops on himself. He said he called them because he thought they were going to come over and counsel us.

"Counsel us? They are cops, not counselors," then banged

on him.

I couldn't believe what I heard. This dude was clearly smoking something that was giving him a chemical imbalance.

Sly called back, but I turned off my phone and tried to go to sleep. I wanted to let go of Sly all together, but I didn't know how. I truly felt like a "bag lady." I had that song by Erykah Badu on repeat all night.

The next morning, I decided to visit a church my sister told me about. Christ Like, under the leadership of Bishop David C. Glover and his wife, Pastor Kandice Glover.

When I went to the church, I felt the presence of the Lord. It was a feeling I hadn't felt in a long time.

The topic of the message was "Let God turn your hurt into God's glory." The pastor said we can't trust our five senses because our flesh will tell us something contrary to what God is telling us.

For instance, if you lose your job or live paycheck-to-paycheck, the devil might tell you that you are broke and that you're going to be broke for the rest of your life and you will lose everything. If your faith is not strong, you will start making stupid decisions because you are scared. But the reality is, this is only a process that God wants you to go through so when you come up, God's glory will be revealed in your life.

The same people who saw you broke, busted, and disgusted will see you prosper because trouble does not last always. But you have to believe in God and see past what you see, and those who see you suffer will see you reign.

Most millionaire ideas were birthed when the person was broke, but they believed the impossible and kept striving. They kept their eyes on the picture that others could not see.

They tapped into that sixth sense, which is faith. As a Christian, you have to walk by faith and not by sight because without faith, it is impossible to please God. Besides, if you don't have faith, you are going to have fear. Fear will torment you and kill you slowly because all fear is false evidence appearing to be real.

Sometimes what you see and hear will mess you up because it is your now situation, but it is not your future. If you allow fear to infiltrate you, you will never see or experience the mind-blowing experience that God has in store for you.

You have to go through the unavoidable process. Weeping may endure for the night, but joy will come in the morning.

We as humans do what feels good to our flesh and look for a quick fix. Everything that feels good to us is not good for us.

For example, some of us have the evidence of a feel-good experience running around the house right now. As you are reading this right now, you are telling Baby Cakes, Cool Breeze and Droopy Draws to sit down somewhere and be quiet. You are struggling to make ends meet and your baby dads definitely aren't helping you. You can't find them and child support can't find them neither. This is what happens when you have children by drug dealers or men who don't have a legit job. They disappear.

The pastor said, "Let your hell experience push you to holiness."

He said you have to trust God and "let your faith fight through your flesh," and that you have more promises from God than problems. There is nothing too hard for God.

During the sermon, I felt that thing in my soul. Though I have two kids by two different men, I knew that I could trust God to help me with my bills. I didn't have to sleep with Sly or any other man to get my bills paid.

I made a decision to trust God because I knew with certainty that God would take care of me and my children. Besides, how could I go wrong with the Lord on my side?

I realized that respect goes so much further than a wet behind because God fearfully and wonderfully made me.

The restoring of my self-respect was the beginning of my restitution. I figured out that no one is going to love me more than me. I owed true love to myself and my children. On that Sunday, I decided to cherish and protect my self-love. I looked at it as my treasure and that no more was I going to give what is sacred to dogs or cast my pearls to pigs. If you do they may trample them under their feet and turn and tear you to pieces. That is what I had been allowing Sly to do to me. *My pearls are precious because God said so*, and that's in the Book read it. Matthew Chapter 7 verse 6.

I was so hyped after church.

Chapter 16
Sister Talk

Diamond brought Big Boy back that afternoon. Tomorrow would be his first day of school. My Big Boy is in first grade. He was so excited, and so was I.

I told her about all the drama that happened between Sly and me.

"Why didn't you call me?" she asked.

"There was no need to. Sis, I miss him so much. I miss the loving so bad that it hurts, but I keep saying to myself this is all worth it."

Diamond said, "Sis, you have to find that inner strength to leave him alone completely."

"I told her sometimes I cry for hours because I feel my body calling him in the middle of the night. My mind is telling me no, but my body is telling me yes."

"Okay, R. Kelly," Diamond said.

"I'm telling you, now I know what R. Kelly was talking about," I said.

We chuckled.

"How did Sly get his truck?" Diamond asked.

"Sis, I don't know because he hasn't called me, and I haven't called him."

"When was the last time you been with him on that level,"

she asked.

"I really can't remember because we been so off and on for so long," I answered.

"Sis, your problem is you are entirely too emotional and you want to be boss. If you feel that you are not number one, you go crazy. Sly is what I consider a *worthless emotion* because each of his other women is number one when he is with them. The same thing that he is telling you, he tells them chicks. On the flip side, some of his chicks just want to smash with no strings attached. That's how coquettes or hoes move, whatever you want to call them. They all f@#$ for a buck they are knavish. Sis, adapt this mind-set: Sly is only your baby dad. When you two smash, it is just on that level, and that's it. If you do this, then you will be good. You want that feeling of entitlement with Sly. But real talk, Sly doesn't care. He is very insecure. Any man that hits, and mentally or emotionally abuses a woman is very insecure. He is one step away from a fag because he is trying to prove something to himself—that he's not in the closet."

"Sis, now you just had an R. Kelly moment," I said.

"Real talk, sis. Remember this; a man that hits women is a misogynist."

"In lay man's terms please," I said.

She said, "Sis," being short, "he hates women and go find yourself."

"You really think Sly might be on the DL?"

"There's a thin line between a pimp and a faggot. He has

all those kids and don't take care of them. For real, what is he trying to prove?" Diamond said.

I responded, "That he is irresponsible."

"I told you all of this, but you are still not going to leave him until you really get good and tired," she continued. "Plus, you are too horny. But real talk, I think Sly gave you that philtre. That's why I only mess with that quaffer, sis. You know what I'm saying," in her ghetto voice.

Diamond always had a passion for saying words that you don't hear every day; she had like a peculiar obsession with them.

She went on to say, "Being that you don't want to mess with somebody else, you will be right back with him."

"Dag, sis. That's how you feel?"

"Yep, because it's real," she replied. "You are my one and only sister, and I know you like I know the back of my ass. Though I wash my ass every day, I damn sure don't look at it."

"Sis, what is wrong with you?" I asked.

"You know we a little off. That's why you with Sly," said Diamond. "Another thing I know: you are strong willed, but once your mind is made up, it is made up for good, bad, or indifferent."

"Yeah, you are right. When I decide to leave this dude, I'm going to shock the hell out of everybody, even him."

"Remember when we used to walk home from school?" Diamond asked. "Dad would tell us not to deviate, go straight home, and you would not for nothing. I, on the other hand, would go to the store, steal some candy, hang out with my friends, and somehow we would end up at the house at the same time. You always were the good child. You followed directions no matter what. If someone told you not to do something, you wouldn't do it. Me, I would do it just because they told me not to, because I was curious and I needed to know the outcome.

"I said all that to say that you been with Sly's sambo, cheating ass for seven years and never cheated on him, still love him, still being patient, and still believing in him to change. She said you would see him dead before you sleep with another dude. That is something I just can't comprehend. Furthermore, you won't even mess with somebody else when you are not with him."

Yelling now, she said, "Sis, it is not cheating when you're not together. Stop being that good girl because Sly doesn't care about how good you are to him. Be in the majority and mess with somebody else. There are no females in this world like you that love this hard."

"Yes, there are."

"Well," Diamond said, "I damn sure don't want that kind of love. I will continue to stick with my liking you a lot theory, the same way I like you is the same way that I don't have to like you. It is so much easier, and nobody gets hurt at the end of the day."

"How am I going to get him out of my system?" I asked desperately.

Diamond responded, "Well, you did go to church today?"

"Yes, I did."

"Well, since you do everything by the book, pray about it.

Maybe you will get the desired results you're looking for because only God can change your mind and heart. Yeah, do that because you need tout de suite divine intervention in this situation."

I responded, "Vincitomnia veritas, and that's Latin now go figure."

She responded, "Yasss, sis. Good one. Sauve qui peut, and that's the shit I'm on."

I chuckled and said, "Oui."

"When did you learn French?" I asked.

"Like I told you before," Diamond said. "I take God everywhere I go and I mean everywhere."

Then I responded, "Let me find out you be in France."

We laughed then switching back to my regular tone.

"I wish this was just that easy, but we know God is not a wizard with this magical wand who says this magical line and—poof!—all of our troubles are gone. This thing right up and through here is going to take more than praying. Today, the bishop said some things only come through prayer and fasting."

Diamond said, "I don't know about the not-eating part, but as of now, you already been fasting from sex. Not getting it for five and six months at a time is a fast in my book. That's that new fast—F-A-S-T. F is for *finally*, A is for *asking*, S is for *Sly* or *someone Else*, and T is for *to do it*. FAST!"

"I thought you didn't like Sly?"

"I don't, but I be feeling your pain. If Sly does the job for you, then you need to stop depriving yourself. Just make sure he uses protection because I don't want a tribe called quest of nieces and nephews," Diamond said.

"Something is really wrong with you," I said. "But real talk, if I do give Sly some, then I will be back to square one, and me and the kids deserve so much better."

"Sex with Sly is just sex, and that's it," Diamond said. "But when you go Molly and add the kids, that's when it becomes complex. Basically, I'm saying just smash without any emotion and don't give him your heart because that he doesn't deserve. And besides, you had a child for him and that's more than enough."

"Sis, I wish I knew how to do that."

Diamond said, "Take off the blonde wig and try it. I'm telling you, it will work. Remember, take the emotion out."

"I hear you, sis, but I'm not feeling it because it seems to me that if I do that, then I will start to become bitter in my heart. Eventually, I will have no love in my heart. If I become bitter, how can I effectively raise my children in genuine love? Don't you think that will trickle down to my children and then they will become angry, bitter, and hateful? I don't want little Twinkle's and Sly's in training, running around because they are not going to be able to give love or receive love because I was feeding them that fruit of bitterness. Without love, I'm nothing.

Sis, when I finally heal from Sly, I will have to try to reprogram my kids to love again. I'm afraid that by then it's going to be harder, and I might not be successful because they will be grown. I have to think about how many lives they will hurt because of their pain. Hurting people hurt people."

I started thinking about how the Bible instructs us to train up a child in the way he should go and when he is old he will not depart from it.

"Sis," I continued, "I have to train them right because if I don't, their blood will be on my hands. Nah, sis, I'm not going to let Sly's germs infiltrate in my house. Somebody has to be the bigger and the better person. That somebody is going to be me."

Diamond said, "There goes that goody-two-shoes attitude you have."

"It might sound corny, but I'm going to break the generational curses of abuse, anger, hate, rage, bitterness, lies, low self-esteem, substance abuse and lust," I said. "Somebody has to do it, and it's going to be me."

"Dang, church did something to you today."

"Yes. It was life changing, One Sunday you should come with me."

"I keep telling you I go to church every day because I take God everywhere I go. And on that note, I'm out."

"It's funny when you start asking people to come to church they want to leave all of a sudden. Thank you for watching Big Boy. We will connect on a later date."

Chapter 17
Mixed Emotions

The next day, Shaquan started first grade. Every day since then, he had a story about what happened in school. One day, I received a letter from his teacher stating that he had been nominated to be in the accelerated math competition. He excelled in math and was very excited he got picked. When I say he studied hard, he studied hard, every night for a week. I helped him every night with his math review.

A day before the competition, I received a summons in the mail from the state of New Jersey stating that they charged Sly with terroristic threats. His court date was October 25.

The same day I received the summons, Shaquan asked if Sly could come to his math contest. I said let's call and ask him. Sly didn't answer when I called, but he called right back. Shaquan picked up.

"What's up? I have a math contest tomorrow, and I want to know if you can come."

When he hung up, he told me that Sly was coming over.

I told Shaquan that you didn't tell Sly what time the contest started, so we'd have to call him back, but Sly beat us to the punch.

I answered this time.

"Shaquan is doing his thing in school," he said. "He's got it like that because he has a smart mom."

"You damn right, by the way, I received a summons in the mail, and you have to go to court on October 25 because the state pressed charges on you."

He asked if I could go to court with him, and I told him that I would try.

Then I asked why didn't they mail the summons to you? He admitted that he gave the court my address. I asked him why did he do that.

"Babe, I miss you and my kids. I will be over tomorrow morning to go to Shaquan's contest."

"Yeah, he forgot to tell you that the contest is from 10:00 to 10:30."

Sly said he'd be at the house around nine.

"Okay, I will see you tomorrow, and we will ride together."

Being flirtatious, Sly repeated "We riding together!"

"Let me go because I have to feed Baby Girl," I said while brushing him off. "We'll see you in the morning."

Shaquan was so hyped about his math contest that he wanted to go to bed right after dinner. I told him to wait at least a couple of hours.

After he went to bed, I started thinking about who was going to watch Baby Girl when I went back to work. Pricy would be ideal, but I didn't know how consistent she would be. I started feeling overwhelmed, so I started to drink some red wine. I couldn't smoke because I was breastfeeding. The wine led to shots of Hennessy.

What the hell, I already had breast milk prepared for Baby Girl. If worse comes to worse, I would drink a lot of water later.

After a few shots, I started to feel right; the house was quiet, and I had my old school jams on. I was in Twinkle's world feeling good, and then our song came on, "Before I Let You Go" by Black Street.

I started to miss Sly, and I thought about calling him. *But why should I call him? He knows where I'm at.* I kept drinking my Henny and imagined Sly and me making another baby. Damn, where is he when I need him? A few minutes later, my doorbell rang. Guess who it was?

When I opened the door, he said, "VP, you been drinking?"

I didn't answer his question; I had one of my own. "What the hell are you doing here?"

"I thought I would surprise you and come tonight."

"You know I have a restraining order against you," I said.

"I know, but I don't care."

I just imagined this dude up.

He sat down and asked, "Is this what you do now? Drink?"

I ignored him.

"Aren't you breastfeeding my baby?" he asked.

"Yeah."

"So I guess my baby is drinking Henny too."

"Sly, stop acting so damn concerned. You have nine baby moms, and they are all crackheads, and you trippin' because I'm drunk. Boy, you have your priorities messed up." I chuckled.

"I'm glad you think it's funny."

"What's funny is the fact that I didn't invite your ass over here tonight. You only surfaced because you think I'm screwin' somebody."

"Twinkle, why are you trying to start?"

"Because I can, as a matter of fact, take them off."

"VP, you are drunk, and we are in the living room."

"I know where we are at. This is my house. Take them off, Sly. What, you shy now?"

"You want it like this," he said.

"Forget it, Sly. You are talking too much. I'll take my shit off."

So I started to remove my jeans and panties.

"Isn't this what you want?" I asked.

"Yeah," he said.

I got on top of him and started grinding him. "Take them off," I repeated and unbuttoned and unzipped his pants.

I started riding him hard and fast.

"This is what you want, right?" I asked.

"Baby, slow down and kiss me," he said.

"No. You like it like this, don't you?"

He told me to slow down again. I refused and started riding him harder and faster until he forcefully pushed me off of him. I fell to the floor.

"Why are you f@#$%$# me like a trick?" He was yelling

as he stood and zipped his pants. "What has gotten in you?"

"You and your demons, that's what gotten in me."

"Baby, I'm sorry for hurting you."

I started screaming, "I hate you, Sly."

"What have I done to you?" Tears welled in his eyes. "You are becoming a different person. Now you can't even love me like you used to."

"I do hate you, I hate your guts. I hate you for abusing and crushing my heart, and now I don't have one. I hate the fact that I will be connected to you for the rest of my life."

"Twinkle, don't let my mess-ups make you a person that you are not."

Sly lifted me off the floor. I tried to fight him off, but he just held me tighter.

"Twinkle, f@#$ me up, but my kids need you."

It seemed like he held me so tight that he squeezed the tears out of me. I couldn't stop them.

"Cry," he said. "Let all that shit out."

"Why do you always hurt me? Why do you take my heart and rip it out of me and then step and spit on it?"

"Baby, I'm sorry. I'm so sorry. Don't become this hateful person that you are not. Twinkle, I need help. I don't know how to be faithful. I come from generations of womanizers. I don't want to be one, but something inside of me drives me to do it. Baby, this is something inside of me I can't control."

He held me for a few moments.

"One thing I know is that I love you and never loved any woman ever before. I fell in love with you because I recognized the love you have for your son and now my daughter. I don't know how to protect and cherish love the way I'm supposed to. Baby, my kids need that sweet, loving, honest, healthy person that I know you are."

I cried some more.

"Twinkle, promise me something."

"What is it," I asked as tears streamed down my face.

"Promise me that no matter what goes on with us that you will always be strong."

I nodded.

"Now wash your face and go to bed," he said.

Sly slept in the living room and didn't bother me. I think he was concerned of what he thought I was becoming. It messed him up, and he blamed himself.

I started to understand that in Sly's eyes I was his angel, steady lover, and supportive anchor. He respected, admired, and cherished me regardless if he was around or not. Me being out of character disturbed him greatly.

Sly could smash all the chicks he wanted to, but when it came to us making love, he wanted to feel passion. He didn't want me to be like the other chicks. I'm special and different in Sly's eyes.

Sly woke me up at 5:15 a.m. I asked why he slept in the living room. He said he had a lot on his mind, and he needed to think.

"Twinkle, you are so much better than that. The love I have for you can't compare to what I feel for those other females. Promise me that you won't allow me to make you bitter."

We kissed and made love.

He whispered in my ear, "Lisa, don't let me make you crazy. Promise me this while I'm making love to you that no matter what I do, you will stay focused."

"Baby, why are you saying this?" I asked.

"Because as bad as I don't want to hurt you, I can't promise you that I won't. I don't know how to heal you because I never was healed from my own hurt and pain."

"Baby, we can heal together," I answered.

"Teach me and don't give up on me," he responded.

I said, "I won't give up on you or us."

That morning was deep. I couldn't stop thinking about what Sly told me.

Baby Girl woke up. Sly changed her and fed her the prepared bottles. Then Big Boy woke up. He was excited to see Sly. His breakfast was a turkey sausage, egg, and cheese sandwich.

Before he walked to the bus stop, he asked, "Mom, can we pray that I win the math contest."

"Sure."

We all held hands. I prayed and told Shaquan to believe God.

"I do, Mom, because my sister is here and Sly is too. I'm

going to win this thing."

"Yes, you are."

I gave him a kiss, and Sly walked him to the bus stop.

When Sly returned, he said, "VP, I love you and my family. No matter what, always remember that."

"I love you back, baby."

We got dressed, and we were sharp. Yes, I know we were only going to Big Boy's contest, but that's how we did it.

We arrived at the school at 9:45 a.m. and walked into the auditorium. We got good seats. When Shaquan walked in, I started cheering real loud and didn't care what anybody was going to say about my loud ass.

There were twenty kids in the contest. They were asked addition, multiplication, and subtraction problems. Whoever hit the buzzer first was able to answer the question. To make this long story shorter my son won!

Sly was so ghetto. You know that loud whistle you do with your two fingers? That's what he did. We didn't even care. I was so proud of Shaquan. He was so proud of himself.

We left and stopped to get lunch before returning home.

"That little boy has always been competitive," Sly said.

"I know," I said, but I had been thinking about other things. "Baby, I think we should start going to church together."

"You can go, but I don't mess with the boy like that."

"What boy? Jesus?" I asked.

He said, "Yeah."

"Maybe you should start. You know you will be going to court in about a week and will need all the prayers you can get. Just think about it."

"If it's going to better me, then maybe I will try," he said. "Where is the church?"

"It's about ten minutes away in a garage and the name of it is Christ Like," I answered.

"A garage," he asked.

"Yes, and don't let the garage fool you because remember the boy Jesus was born in a manger where horses and cattle ate."

"True! True!" he said. "Twinkle, that's real."

"I know, right? That is something to think about. But I really think that you will enjoy the service."

"When are you going again?" he asked.

"This Sunday."

"I don't know about going this Sunday."

"Why? You scared of the boy Jesus?" I responded.

He replied, "Twinkle, get out of here."

"Yeah, that's what I thought. If you scared, say you scared. Negro, just man up. A lot of people are scared of him just for the simple fact we ain't never seen him. The unknown messes with people's psyche. But we sure can feel his presence. Just like we can't see air, but we know without it we will die. Just look at it as Jesus being the breath of life. Oh yeah, and we are going this Sunday. I said so Saturday you can stay the night so you will already be here."

"That sounds good," Sly said.

"I bet you it does," I responded.

When Shaquan got home, I told him I was going to treat him for doing such a wonderful job and winning the contest. He could have whatever he wanted for dinner.

He said he wanted General Tso chicken with shrimp fried rice and to beat Sly in chess.

"You got it."

That evening Shaquan got everything he wanted. Sly also took him to the mall and got him a few outfits, while Baby Girl and I stayed home and chilled. That night, Sly stayed late, but he didn't stay, and I was good with it. When he left, he told me he would be back later.

When Saturday came around, Sly showed up with his church clothes. We had fun. As usual, he cooked. In the middle of the night, he tended to Baby Girl.

Sunday morning, I could tell that Sly was nervous. We got dressed and went to church. He was feeling the service, and I noticed he got teary eyed.

He leaned over and whispered, "Babe, I'm starting to feel the ghost."

"Good, babe, let go and let God have his way."

He looked at me as if he was saying, "Okay, V.P."

I knew he was worried about his court date.

Sly was enjoying the service. He was nodding his head and clapping his hands during praise and worship. He even got up during the altar call. He repeated the sinner's prayer and had the courage to join the church. I hadn't joined the church yet.

"I'm looking at this dude like you really joined the church without me. Isn't that something we are supposed to discuss? I mean we are not married, but we are engaged."

After service, it seemed like every member of the congregation shook his hand and showed him love.

Back in his truck, I had to check his reasons.

"I felt like that was something I needed to do," he replied.

"Isn't that something we are supposed to discuss?" I asked.

"VP, I didn't even think about it because I didn't know I was going to join. Why? Are you mad?"

"No, I'm not mad, Sly. I am glad you made such a positive step," I told him.

I wanted to add, *Maybe you'll stop hustling and get a real job now*, but I kept that to myself.

We got home and relaxed for a bit before Sly cooked a bangin' Sunday dinner. He made fried and baked chicken, mac and cheese, collards, yams, and a chocolate cake. My baby knew how to throw down, and I loved every bit of it. So did Big Boy and Baby Girl. We all love to eat.

Later that night, Sly was being real quiet. I asked if he was okay. He said he was just thinking. I asked about what.

"When you go back to work, who is going to watch my daughter?" he asked.

"I'm not sure, but it's going to work itself out," I said.

"I'm a little worried about my court date."

"I know, but that too is going to work out as well," I said.

"Baby, it's all good." He said.

"Yes, it is."

Chapter 18

Got Him

We had to be at court by nine thirty in the morning for Sly's hearing. He didn't consult an attorney. Why, I don't know. I guess he thought he had chump charges that he could beat.

They called Sly's name, and he walked to the front of the room. The judge asked if he had an attorney present. A public defender stood and said he was representing him. Then the judge stated that Sly was facing terroristic threat charges. Based on his "scary criminal history" of domestic violence, armed robbery, drug trafficking, terroristic threats, and kidnapping, the judge said he didn't want Sly in his town.

The public defender interjected and asked if he could have a word with his client. The public defender negotiated that Sly would do thirty days in county jail and take anger management counseling.

The judge told Sly if he didn't finish the anger management sessions while he was locked up, he could do between two and five years. My heart dropped. Sly looked at me as the officers took him away. I went home and waited for Sly's phone call.

Finally he called. He said everything was going to be okay. Thirty days was really no time to him because he did twenty-four months in 1988.

I asked him what he wanted me to do. He told me to let his

brother know what was going on. I did as he requested.

BM got smart with me and said it was my fault.

"Look, BM, I wasn't the one who called the cops. Your brother did," I said then hung up.

Sly called me and ask me to go up there and bring him underwear and to give him money for cigarettes. After two and a half weeks, I was getting tired of visiting him. I had to take Baby Girl with me, and it was too much. She was only two months and some change, and I was exposing her to all those nasty germs in the jail. So in one visit, I told Sly that I wouldn't be able to come back if I didn't find someone to watch Baby Girl. He only had about two more weeks.

He got mad and cussed me out and told me not to come back. I told Sly that he didn't say nothing but a word because I didn't want to come anyway. The jail was nasty, and it smelled just like sin. The atmosphere wasn't for me or my baby.

Two weeks went by, and I didn't hear from Sly. However, I knew he was out because my home-girl worked at the jail and told me.

I would be returning to work next week and still didn't know who was going to watch Baby Girl. I couldn't find Pricy anywhere.

I decided to take Baby Girl and Shaquan to Philly to see Sly's mom. She had called me before he got locked up and told me that she wanted to see her granddaughter.

When I arrived, Sly's sister, Dorian, opened the door.

"Why you are here, Twinkle?" she asked.

Calmly I answered, "So your mom can see her granddaughter."

"We don't care about your kids, and we don't want you here at our house."

Mind you I'm holding Baby Girl and Big Boy is standing beside me.

Then she went on to say that I tried to take her brother's freedom away because he didn't want me and he has millions of women.

"Who do you think you are talking to?" I asked.

"You," she said and slammed the door.

I took the kids to the car and put Baby Girl in her car seat. I told Big Boy I'd be back and to keep the car door locked. He knew not to open it for anybody unless they knew our secret password.

"Mom, what are you going to do?" he asked.

"Take care of unfinished business."

I knocked back on the door, and Dorian answered.

"Bitch, now what were you saying?" I yelled.

She shouted, "Twinkle, I don't have time to argue back and forth with you. Take this shit to my brother's house."

"I'm bringin' it here first, and then I will deal with your brother."

She opened the screen door a little, and I warned her if that door touched me, I was going to hurt her.

"I don't care that you are six foot four inches and five

hundred pounds. As a matter of fact, bring your fat ass outside so you will know firsthand how I beat your punk-ass brother's ass."

"Whatever," she said.

"It wasn't whatever a minute ago when you disrespected me in front of my kids," I hollered.

"You disrespected my brother," she yelled.

"Your stupid-ass brother called the cops on himself," I screamed. "Before you come at me, know what the hell you are talking about."

Then she slammed the door and called the police. They arrived while I was still banging on the door. I thought to myself, these punks love calling the law but don't follow the law. The officers asked me to leave.

I was so mad that I drove to Sly's apartment. Of course, he wasn't there. I went home. I figured he would call me when his sister tells him what happened.

When I got home, I called my sister. She was so down to go over there and do a drive-by. When it came to her big sis, she was ready on demand. Diamond came through and stayed a while at my apartment.

"What is it going to take for you to leave him alone altogether," she said.

"Sis, I'm going to do it. I promise you."

The phone rang. It was Pricy asking when I was going back to work. I told her Monday, and she said she'll be over Sunday night.

"Don't play because if you don't show up, there will be a situation because you'll be messing with my money."

"I got you, Twinkle. Are going to church tomorrow?"

"Yes, do you want to go with me?"

"Nah, I was just making sure you were going."

"Chick, you got the audacity."

"I sure do," she said and hung up the phone.

To my surprise, Diamond said, "I might go. If I do, I will meet you there."

"Sounds good to me," I responded.

"I'm about to leave."

"Okay, thanks, sis. Possibly, I will see you tomorrow."

"Like I told you before," she said. "I take Jesus everywhere I go."

"Well, take him to church with you tomorrow," I said as she went out the door.

As soon as I shut the door, the phone rang. It was Sly.

"What's up?"

"Twinkle, why did you get smart with my sister?"

"Because she tried to play me in front of our kids, I guess she thought I was a dumb broad who didn't care about my kids. What would you have done if you saw me beating her fat ass?"

"You are so rude, but I probably would have had a heart attack."

"That's what you would of have had then. Just like you get the business, so can she, I ain't no respecter of persons."

We laughed.

"You know how my sisters are."

"Yeah, and now they know how the girl Twinkle is. I've never been scared of you and damn sure ain't scared of your sisters. And why are you calling?"

"Because I want to go to church with you tomorrow."

"Weren't you just mad at me," I asked.

"No, you were the one mad. Since you didn't want to come up there, I just told you not to."

"Okay, Sly."

"Babe, I'm not worried about you and my sister."

"Me neither."

Sly said he'd be over around 10:30 p.m. that night. It was closer to 1:30 a.m. When he arrived he smelled like the bar, chicken wings and cheap perfume.

I had romance on my mind, but now I was thinking, *Here we go again.* I let him in, and I went back to bed.

"What's up?" he asked.

"Sleep, and don't be so loud because you might wake up Anisa."

"Oh, that's how it's going down tonight? I ignored him."

The next morning Sly tried to get some, and if looks could kill, he would have died right then. As we were getting ready for church, he asked when I was starting work.

"Tomorrow," I answered.

"Who's going to watch my daughter?" Sly asked.

I told him Pricy.

"Doesn't she smoke that stuff?" he asked.

"You like smokers, so what's the problem?"

Appearing to be concerned, Sly asked. "What if she gets high around my baby?"

"Sly, are you going to watch her? Oh no, because you sell crack. So who is worse, the dealer or the addict? And all your baby moms are smokers, and you don't trip on them. They were getting high carrying your baby, selling their diapers and clothes after they had the baby, and you talking about my cousin. Joker, please. Before you point the finger, remember you have three pointing right back at you. And one thing I know is that my cousin will never put her family in danger. She loves me too much."

"Smokers don't have no love."

"I guess you are talking from experience," I replied.

He walked out the room and started talking to Big Boy. I rolled my eyes.

Sly drove to church. The service was fiya. The topic of the message was "Keep It Real with Yourself."

The bishop preached about judging others and said, "In the same way you judge others, you will be judged."

He said that after you do inventory on yourself, you will begin to have compassion on others because we all have some mess in us. Each person has to face their demons and stop looking at everybody else's faults.

We all have sinned and fallen short of the glory of God, he said. If anyone says they have not sinned, that person is saying God is a liar. His word is not in that person. Bottom line no one is perfect, but we are striving for perfection. End of Story!

He said you must forgive yourself so you can forgive others.

This bishop is gangsta, I thought. He kept it all the way 100.

After church, Sly stayed for a little while. I was okay with him leaving early because church was good and I felt full. It also gave me time to prepare for work.

I knew in my heart it was over between us because when he wasn't here I felt free. When he came around, there was a heavy weight on me. As if, he was a black cloud hovering over me. Somehow, I felt like he was blocking my blessings.

I changed my prayer. Instead of asking God to remove Sly, I asked God to change my mind-set and give me the strength to leave Sly for good. I remember my grandma preaching about letting this mind be in you which is also in Christ Jesus. I decided that I'd rather be hurt and be in God's will then be hurt without him. Being in the will of God is the safest place.

Although he was going to church, I believed his intentions were not genuine. When he was telling me he couldn't promise he wouldn't hurt me again, he was asking for a free cheat card. I know what I said when we were doing what lovers do, but I was thinking with a clear mind now. Having sex gets your emotions cloudy. Sly was a master manipulator, and the more I prayed about him, the more I saw myself and him for who he really was. What people fail to realize, is people can manipulate you, but they can't manipulate the God in you. I don't care how slick they think they are. *They are not that slick.*

Pricy arrived around 8:30 p.m. We talked for a couple hours. She shared that she was really trying to get clean. She had picked up some weight, and she was looking real cute in the face.

I think Pricy loved me the most because, out of all the cousins, I looked like her the most.

I crashed out early because you know how the first day back to work can be. Adjusting to the work flow can be a bit tiresome.

The next morning, I told Pricy all of the things I needed done. We both knew she had to keep busy so she wouldn't start itching.

I drove Big Boy to the bus stop. He wanted to wait in the car for his bus. We talked briefly. His bus came, and he gave me a kiss and told me to have a good day at work.

I told him to have a good day at school as well and gave him another kiss and a tight hug. He was so thoughtful.

I arrived at work. It felt like I never left, and I picked up right where I left off.

Around noon, I checked in with Pricy. Baby Girl was good, and she said she was doing good.

When I got home, Pricy told me Sly called to check up on Anisa. I said to myself, he didn't call me all day. I felt a shade of secrecy.

I asked her how long they talked. She said five minutes. *That's a long time*, I thought, but I just shook it off. I knew Pricy is street breed and so is Sly.

Pricy took a lot of the load off me, which was a good look.

As time went on, Sly would come over to see the kids, and he would give me some money, but that was it. However, on the weekends, he would stay because he would still go to church. He slept in the living room because I was beginning to value my worth as a woman. Say what you want to say. It felt good to keep my precious pearls to myself, and there was no drama.

Pricy would usually leave on Fridays after I got home from work and would come back on Sunday evenings around eight.

Sly would always have something negative to say about Pricy watching *his* daughter, like Anisa wasn't my daughter too.

Sly would talk just to hear himself talk, and I would be looking at him like shut up. I told him that in spite of how he feels about Pricy, she does everything I ask her to do and more. She loves Anisa, Shaquan, and me. I should have told him to find someone else if he was that upset about it. It's funny how people have so much to say about a problem but won't be the solution to the problem. *That's some nerve.*

Chapter 19

Deuces

One Saturday night, Sly asked, "Twinkle, what's up? Lately you haven't been giving me any."

I gave him the gas face and said you will get some when we get married.

"By the way," I paused, "when are we getting married?"

Sly replied, "I don't know. But whenever we do, Anisa has to be old enough to be the flower girl."

Mind you, Anisa is five months old.

"About how long?" I said.

Agitated, Sly responded, "Why are you pressuring me? You have a ring."

"Yeah, I do, but I'm too old for friendship or commitment rings."

"I think in another five years."

"Another five years." I was mad instantly.

"Sly, we've been together for damn near seven years and you want to wait for another five years? Now I get it. You just want to keep stringing me along and keep using me until you get tired or until I get tired. Well, listen to this; I made a conscious decision not to have sex with you or anybody else until I get married because if sex is our foundation, our marriage will never work. So we may as well save our time, money and energy because I'm realizing we don't have a solid foundation. All we have is a compatible sex life, and real talk, it's getting old. I'm not even feeling it like that."

Now Sly was enraged. "Oh, it's getting old, Twinkle!" he yelled.

"Yes!" I yelled back.

Then Sly started fussing about being tired of the back and forth and my procrastination.

"Sly, you heard the preached word just like I did. The Bible clearly states that sex is honorable only in marriage and God will judge the whoremongers and adulterers.

"Well, you should have thought about that before you had Anisa."

"Oh! Anisa is a free pussy pass to you? Anisa should have made you think about doing things right. Clearly you really don't love your family. My soul is more important to me than your international dick anyway. Sly, how can you hear the bishop preach about fornication and how the act is more than a physical act and how souls connect and form ungodly soul ties and ignore the message? Church is not a buffet. You just don't pick out what you want and leave the rest. It's all or nothing, Sly."

Sly responded, "What am I supposed do?"

"Do what you've been doing. You were smashing chicks when I was smashing you anyway. For real…for real, nothing really changed with you, and I ain't beat. Do you, Sly! But as for me and my house, we will serve the Lord. I will not be double-minded or unstable in my ways because that is for the Alpacas.

I've been asking God to change me and the way I think. Finally, I feel my help coming."

"Well, I'm not going to stay the night tonight. And I won't be going to church tomorrow."

"I don't care because serving and loving God is personal anyway," I said.

"I'm going to do me."

"I'm going to do God," I replied. "Deuces."

Then he left.

At church, I praised and worshipped God. I prayed for His help in my new walk of celibacy because I loved Sly and loved to have sex with him. I knew this walk was going to be hard as heck.

I truly wanted to walk upright before God, not man.

Sly was the only man I had been with since I was nineteen years old. I was aware that the more intimate you become with a person, the tighter the ungodly bond becomes. I knew it was going to be hard to detach.

Sly and I were joined as one because every single time an unmarried person has sex, they become illegally married to that person in the spirit. They illegally plant seeds in each other's garden. Remove those unfruitful seeds.

"Therefore a man shall leave his father and his mother and shall cleave unto his wife, and they shall be one flesh." God made sex for marriage only, and marriage should be honored by both parties. I will tell you this, before you get married, please make sure that those ungodly soul ties are destroyed by both parties. If the ungodly soul ties are not destroyed, I can almost guarantee you that someone is going to step outside of the marriage. And both parties are going to encounter major heartache and devastating pain. This is why the divorce rate is so high. Most people chose to marry over there issues because they didn't want to address them before they got married. Just because you got married doesn't mean your prior issues went away or that you were even ready to get married. Now that perverted ghost or whatever ghost you battle with of your past has surfaced in your marriage, and it's haunting and torturing the both of y'all. Pray the ghosts of your past away in Jesus Name and LIVE and declare the works of the Lord. The marriage bed should be kept pure, but that's another book, another story for another time.

My breaking away was leaving me with a lot of emotional scars and it was hurting me like hell along with Sly. He chose to get over his hurt by sexing more women, drugging, and drinking. But I was determined to fight the good fight of faith.

Fighting was my true nature anyway, but this fight wasn't with my hands and feet. For this fight, my weapons were my praise, worship, prayer, fasting, and reading the Bible. I went back to my roots and was doing what I knew worked because, real talk, can't nobody do you like Jesus. So many of us look for happiness in a man or woman, but if you are not happy with yourself, how do you expect someone else to make you happy? True happiness lies in Christ. You can't be incomplete and expect someone to make you whole. If you're looking for someone to make you happy, you will be miserable for the rest of your life. Love yourself and be happy with yourself.

I resolved to beat the spirit of lust and perversion. Every Sunday I went to church and praised God. I asked God to heal my mind and mend my wounded heart, broken spirit, and diseased soul. I praised God because I remember hearing my bishop tell me that praise is your weapon and that faith comes by hearing. "True worshippers worship him in spirit and in truth."

I started to believe God and believe the things that I couldn't see. I started to be mindful of the people whom I embraced. I avoided all negative people and started to guard my mind, heart, ears, eyes, and, more importantly, my soul. I realized that my soul is a very sensitive entity. I understood that when tied to the wrong person, the results are devastating.

Meanwhile, Pricy and I started praying together. She wasn't ready for church, but she was taking baby steps. She started confessing to me and telling me that some weekends when she went home she would slip up. I knew that she wanted to do the will of God. She desired a closer relationship with God but at the same time she didn't know how to completely "let go" of the people, places and things that were tied to her emotions.

However, I was glad that Pricy was acknowledging and voicing her issues instead of denying them. I knew she would eventually be free from her drug habit.

We all have problems we need to get delivered from, and a

crackhead isn't any worse than a liar. Sin is sin, and that's the bottom line. God hates sin. However, judging people will not change them. Loving them will.

Pricy was trying, and that goes a long way with me. Pricy and I were a lot closer. She stayed with me during the weekends since Sly wasn't there. (I hadn't heard from Sly after three months. He didn't even call to check on the kids.) I didn't force her to go to church with me because I believed she would come when she was ready.

Chapter 20

It's a Wrap

One day, my stomach started to hurt while I was working. I asked if I could leave around lunch. I knew that around noon, Baby Girl was sleep. As I pulled up to my apartment, I saw Sly's truck parked outside. So I parked where the car couldn't be seen.

I prepared myself to see some shit that I didn't want to see. I opened my door quietly. Pricy's jeans and shirt were on the living room floor, but I didn't see her or Sly. The TV and radio was on in my son's room. I removed my stilettos and walked quietly toward his room. Baby Girl was asleep in her crib. I peeked into Shaquan's room and saw Pricy mic-checking Sly. He was standing while she was on her knees. They had the nerve to be listening to Kelly Price "She Was a Friend of Mine."

"Yeah, bitch," Sly said. "I knew this wasn't a good idea you watching my daughter, but it worked out perfectly for me."

Pricy kept mic-checking. He told Pricy to take them off. My heart dropped.

"That wasn't part of our agreement."

"I don't care." He opened his hand and revealed a piece of crack. "If you want this rock, then take them off."

Pricy said, "Sly, don't do this."

Sly grabbed her by her neck and started to rape her. I ran to my room and got my baseball bat. I hit Sly over the head again and again until he was knocked out.

Pricy hollered, "Twinkle, stop you are going to kill him."

"Bitch, if you weren't my cousin. I would f@#$ you up too."

Pricy was crying and apologizing. "I got weak," she said. "Sly came over and flaunted the drugs in my face, and I forgot who he was until he asked me to go to the next level."

"How did you get your clothes off," I asked.

Pricy explained how Sly came over, and she let him in. He said that he was there to see Anisa and that he had talked to you earlier.

"I told him that she was asleep, and he insisted that he stay for a while," she said. "We sat down, and I noticed that he dropped a bag on the floor. I looked at it because I wanted it. Sly told me to come and get it, and when I reached for it, he snatched it. He told me to take my shirt and pants off. I told Sly that you are my cousin and I love you. If I had to smash him for drugs, I don't want any. I told him to leave.

"He said to me, 'Pricy, baby, you don't have to smash me. Just do me.' And then he said, 'Take them off.' I took off my jeans and shirt. Anisa started crying, and Sly went to the room, and then I went back there and put the pacifier back in her mouth. Sly went in Shaquan's room and told me to come and take my bra off. I did it. He started to feel my chest and told me to get on my knees.

"I told Sly that I would only munch him. He unzipped his pants and told me to do what I do. So I did for about five minutes, and then he told me to take them off. That's when he grabbed me and started to rape me."

Anisa started crying. I calmed her down.

Sly started to regain consciousness. "Twinkle, I'm sorry," he apologized. "Pricy seduced me. I just came here to see my daughter."

"If you meant well, you would have called me and told me you were coming over or you would have waited until I got off work."

I turned to Pricy. "How long has this been going on?"

"I swear to you this is the first time."

I told Sly to get the hell out of my house and never come back. Pricy kicked him, and he acted like he was going to hit her back.

"Please make my day, please do it," I said.

I started to take my ring off, and Pricy said, "Twinkle, that ring is worth money. Don't be a fool."

I told her to shut the hell up and put some clothes on because I was tired of looking at her saggy ass.

I shut the front door, got Anisa, and sat down in the living room. Pricy was still crying and apologizing. I was so mad at her, but I knew she had a habit, and I knew Sly was to blame. He was also mad at me because he wasn't getting his way.

It's something how hurt people hurt people.

I asked Pricy to make a promise with me that she would get professional help. She promised and said that she would go to church with me. She knew I wasn't taking no for an answer.

I loved Pricy, and I knew that this situation had to happen so I could leave Sly completely alone for good. All things work together for the good of them that love God. Meaning good and bad things bend together and will work out for your good as long as you love God.

This day was the day my blinders came off. The eyes of my heart began to open. The ties of my soul, started to unloose. And my flesh – eating disease called "lust" slowly began to diminish. I finally faced the reality that when Sly would start arguments and disappear. He was purposefully pissing me off so he could do what he wanted to do. I made a conscious decision not to be the Web's action news, and Sly was not going to be my eye witness news. It was finally over and it was time to" DO SUM'N." That's for my dance hall lovers. On this day, I promised myself that I wasn't settling or making any more excuses for him or for myself. Sly was who he was, and I was warned, and he was still who he was. I thought I could change him, but the reality is I can only change myself.

The streets taught me that the way you meet a man is the same way you're going to leave him, and this is true. This day I decided to stop feeding the spider. Instead of being caught up in the Web, I decided I was going to use the silk from the web for my garment of praise instead of using it for the spirit of heaviness. Silk is known for its enduring quality and is one of the strongest fibers. Strong is who I am.

Chapter 21

Expected End

Let your Sly experience make you wiser than a serpent.

So many of you reading this book are Twinkles—a gleam of light. But in the midst of all of your hurt and pain, you lost your sparkle and feel that all hope is gone.

However, it's still there if you choose to become better and not bitter. The more you heal, the brighter your light will shine.

I encourage you if you don't know Jesus as your personal savior; please repeat the sinner's prayer. All jokes aside, this prayer is real and life changing. I'm very serious about the health of your soul, heart, and mind.

Jesus is the only one that can heal all of your soul diseases. If you allow God to come into your life, he will come instantly.

Now I'm not saying that your situation is going to change immediately, but eventually it will get better. Now when you first become a Christian you are going to be amped. You're going to tell everyone about the goodness of Jesus. You're going to go so hard in the paint; people are going to think that you are a li'l crazy. You are going to stop drinking, smoking, smashin', you are even going to try to stop cursing for a little while. You are going to be "turned up" for Jesus. Your life is going to appear to be wonderful for a little while. I call this the "baby stage."

Eventually, real life is going to start hitting you hard. And when it does you might not be so enthused about Jesus any longer. I call this stage "broken." God wants you to see where your heart is at concerning him. Everyone loves God when God is doing everything for them and spoiling them. But how much will you love and trust God when you feel like he does not love you because things are not going your way? Or when you lose your job? When family members are lying on you? Or when your child is on drugs or in a gang? Or you find out that your husband or wife is cheating on you? Or when someone close to you dies? Or when you're still single and you are tired of saying "no" to what or who you know can hit that right spot. Or when the so-called bishop - elect, pastor or church members are shifty? Or when your friends walk away? And although you are praying things look like they are getting worse and not better.

How much will you love God when people say "Where is your God?" What kind of God will allow you to go through so much hell? "You mine as well go back to what you were doing, because if Jesus was real you would not be going through all of this suffering. I don't even serve Jesus and my life is a blast." Or when people question your relationship with Jesus? Or when you question your relationship with Jesus? How much will you love and trust God then? Will you turn your back on him? Or will you stand firm and say for God I live and for God I will die and no matter what I still love and trust you. No matter how "crazy" I may appear to others.

It is this place I call "broken" when you really find out how great God is because God will not reject a broken and repentance heart. In this place God is building your character and preparing you for greatness all at the same time. Along with giving you the strength to make it through. Your set backs are just set – ups by God for a major comeback. When you come back you're going to be unrecognizable. That's how great your blessing is going to be.

Being a Christian at times can be so overwhelming because you have to learn how to truly walk by faith when obstacles come your way. You might even feel like you are at a place called "agony" when you become a mature Christian because sometimes things appear to go all wrong all at once. I don't know why people think when you become a Christian your life is going to be peachy? I come to tell you, only the true warriors will make it. **No fight no victory.** Weak Christian's will not last. Always remember this. God will not put more on you than you can bear. However, something's you are dealing with you put that drama on your own self. Because you did not trust God.

You might be at a place called "agony" but I promise you if you keep moving forward your next stop will be "destiny." And it will eventually get better. Believe! You have to believe and work your faith as well, but remember that your adversary, the devil, is going to try to get you back on his side. But he is a liar, and I rebuke him right now in the name of Jesus. True story. The devil should have killed you when he had a chance. But he couldn't because God's hand was still upon you whether you knew it or not.

Since the devil did not have his way, then he darn sure can't have it now. For I know the thoughts that I think toward you, "saith the Lord," thoughts of peace and not evil, to give you an expected end. I pray for God's strength and power to withhold you and keep you even when you do not want to be kept. Oh yes! There will come a time when you do not want to be kept. But God is a keeper, and you can do it.

Nothing great comes easy. "Only what you do for Christ will last." This walk is a lifestyle, and you must be strong in the Lord, you can do all things through Christ because his strength is in you. Some days will be good days; some will be bad. Do not beat yourself up if you mess up because God is a forgiving God. Nothing shall separate you from the love of God. Do not let the devil say you can't do it. Do not allow him to convince you to give up because of guilt. There is something wonderful on the other side of your pain. The good book says, "Press toward the mark for the prize of the high calling of God in Christ Jesus." I say again, satan is the father of all lies. He wants you to feel sorry for yourself and cry the woe-is-me story hoping that you will give up. He wants you to blame everyone else for your mistakes. Well it's time for you to take some responsibility.

I do not care what wrong you did, you can't do enough wrong for God not to choose you because you were chosen before the foundations of the earth. But you must go through the inevitable process of pain. You're not damaged goods to Christ, my brother and sister. *Count it all joy when you fall into diverse temptation. Knowing that tribulation works patience and patience experience, and experience hope, and hope makes not ashamed.* Yes! You will fall but get back up. Try harder, do not be in denial, and do not give up. Ask Jesus for forgiveness and his grace, mean it and keep moving forward. Falling is part of your process to becoming what God wants you to be, but falling back to your old ways is not.

I find God to be so amazing because when God blesses you, he even blesses your mistakes. There's a song by Structure called "Anyway" that says, 'I don't deserve it / so unworthy / still you bless me anyway." And for that, I praise God that he didn't let my mistakes kill me. God loves you through the good and the bad. That song by J Moss is right on time and so true. Do not worry about what people are going to say about you because they are going to talk regardless. Do not allow other people's opinions make you someone you're not.

Some of the things you went through, some people lost their minds or literally died in it. You're stronger than you think. You already made it through the worse. How do I know? Because you **SURVIVED.** You didn't come this far on your own. God your Father was and still is with you every step of the way.

Please repeat after me:

Father, I'm a sinner, and I'm sorry for all of the wrong that I have done. I ask that you forgive me from all of my sins. I believe you sent your son, Jesus, to die on the cross for me. I believe on the third day he rose with all power and might. I believe if I confess with my mouth and believe in my heart that I'm saved, I am now saved in Jesus's name. Amen.

Now if you wholeheartedly believe what you just said, welcome to your new life. You just changed your focus to what matters. You are no longer defeated, so stop acting like it. When you said this sinner's prayer, the fight was fixed, and every situation you will face you will be victorious if you continue to trust God. Now your spirit was instantly reborn the moment you said the sinner's prayer.

However, your soul has to be transformed by the renewing of your mind according to the Word of God. Our souls can carry over much spiritual corruption due to our past. That's why believers continue to struggle with sin after accepting Christ. Our soul needs to be washed clean daily. Feed your spirit with the word of God and do not allow your soul to control you. Remember your soul consist of your mind, will and emotions. The real you is your spirit and your body is just a shell or temple that we temporarily live in.

Salvation is free; however, the anointing will cost you a lot of—obedience, tears, pain, being misunderstood. But it's all worth it. The anointing comes from the challenges you've conquered. The anointing is a relationship that you've encountered with God, but it's not until you go through something and conquer it until its power is professed. Perfection comes through suffering.

Something to think about: if you can stay faithful to a man who does not value your worth, you darn sure can stay loyal to a faithful God. When your situation appears to be getting worse, you must believe in God and remain obedient. I pray for deliverance in your life. In order to achieve this, you cannot be in denial; you must stop making excuses and stop blaming everyone else. Execute the excuses and stop settling. Life has too many opportunities to settle.

If you do not have a church home, I encourage you to try hard to find a good one because it's not easy finding the church that will be attached to you, but there is one out there for you. You must stay prayerful while seeking. Once you find that church, please remember the church is a hospital. Do not expect the bishop, the pastor, or the church people to be perfect because we all have issues and struggles and striving for perfection. *No one is exempt from sin. I repeat, no one is.*

Some people in church will get on your last everlasting nerve and some are there on assignment from the devil himself to distract you. God is not calling for organization but salvation. Remember, the world didn't kill you, and don't let church people kill you. **Stay focused on God. You are there for God and not man.** Just trying to help you out before you join. Get the word; get active in the church if you feel that you are ready to do so. Then leave. Do not get caught up in foolishness, cliques or even the hype of it.

The good book says, "But seek ye first his kingdom and his righteousness and all these things shall be added unto you." Always seek God. If you lack wisdom, ask for it. You need Godly wisdom to make it in this wicked world successfully. Once you establish a relationship with God, you will be able to recognize his voice. You will get weak at times, but in your weakness, God's strength is made perfect. Now you must recondition your mind and stop trusting in your five senses and tap into your sixth sense, and that's your faith.

"Faith without works is dead," and you must make it work and work it hard. "Without faith, it is impossible to please God." Faith reveals that God is doing more for his people than we can ever realize through sight alone. When you face difficulties that seem impossible, remember that spiritual resources that you can't see are there. Look with the eyes of faith, and let God show you his resources. If you don't see God working in your life, the problem may be your spiritual eyesight, not God's power.

Everyone has a process, and challenges mature you. Do not miss the miracle because you do not like the process. If you believe that you have an ungodly soul tie, I strongly suggest that you say this prayer, and I promise you this is the last prayer! Wink!

Ungodly soul ties are major; remember the more intimate you become with the individual, the tighter the soul ties becomes.

Now I'm telling you this, you might have to say this prayer a few times a day because this soul tie didn't happen overnight, and depending on the level of intimacy you have with one person or multiple people, it's not going to go away overnight. I'm just being very real.

Ungodly soul ties are formed anytime and every time there is intimacy in a relationship that is outside the will of God. And if you are getting it in like that, those ties are going to be tighter and it's going to be harder for you to detach, but now you can do all things through Christ who strengthens you. You can and will do it if you really want to. I have faith in you. Smile! Yeah, I just had a Kirk Franklin moment. "You look so much better when you smile."

Allow God to have sole custody of your soul because your soul is worth more than you even realize. What do you benefit if you gain the whole world but lose your own soul? The answer is Hell. Your identity is a valuable possession. Protect it. The devil wants your soul, because his job is to rob, steal, kill and destroy. He wants you bound and not free. He wants you to sell your soul, and he wants you to be ignorant about the worth of your soul because he is aware of your soul's authentic value.

Remember he has been around much longer than you and I. He is real and he hates you. He never slacks on his job. Please don't get bamboozled and think that he loves you or even likes you. I repeat he hates you because Jesus loves you. Basically satan is a hater. When your soul is tied to God, there is a divine covering and protection that will enable you to withstand forming ungodly soul ties.

If you believe in God, then you must believe in the devil. You can't believe in one without the other. Yes, I know you did wrong things. So have I, but God is a loving and forgiving God. His grace is sufficient. You deserve the best.

And, yes, I understand that everybody knows how low down and dirty you are, but God did not bless and gift you according to the opinions of people. If the truth be told, we all were a hot mess before God got our attention, and if you catch me on the wrong day I still might be. Look, nobody is perfect; however we are striving for perfection. True confession is good for the soul.

Your actions and your motives must be in line with God. You and God only know the true reason, on why you are doing something. God blesses you when you're doing the right thing for the right motive. He doesn't bless you when you are doing the right thing for the wrong motives. Check your motives. Side bar, you can't manipulate Jesus.

If you can't be honest with yourself and God, you can't be delivered point-blank. You might not be where you want to be, but you darn sure ain't where you used to be. You can't go through life's problems properly without God. Sis / Bro, you need him because he is a heart fixer and a mind regulator— and quoting my Grandma— this too shall pass.

Repeat after me:

I rebuke all sexual sin that I have been involved in within my past and present, even the sin that was no fault of my own through sexual abuse, molestation, and rape. I rebuke all types of addictions, including drugs, alcohol, fornication, masturbation, pornography, perversion, fantasy, idolatry and adultery in the name of Jesus.

I command all spirits of lust and perversion to come up and out of my flesh, stomach, genitals, mind, mouth, eyes, hands, blood, heart, soul, and that of my children and my children's children, in the name of Jesus.

I present my body to the Lord as a living sacrifice holy and acceptable to Him. Now my members are members of Christ. I break ungodly soul ties with former lovers and all sexual partners in the name of Jesus. I cast out all spirits of denial, loneliness, procrastination, instability, vulnerability, insecurity, insanity, fear and low self-esteem that would drive me back to an ungodly sexual relationship in Jesus' precious, powerful, holy name, Amen.

Remember, an ungodly soul tie will be the fruit of the flesh which is lust, perversion, masturbation, addictions, fornication, manipulation, habitual lying, anger, strife, jealously, controlling others, co- dependency, resentment, hatred, confusion, physical abuse, emotional abuse, mental abuse, verbal abuse. It will try to change you into a person you are not by making you feel bad for your positive accomplishments or putting you down to build themselves up.

Basically the reason why men and women put you down and why they have a lot of sexual partners boils down to two things—insecurity and low self-esteem. *It's not because there that horny. It's because they settle for temporary and false attention.*

An ungodly soul tie will keep you from a good relationship with God. It will bring you into spiritual bondage, and if you're not careful, you will slip into idolatry by putting someone or something before God. You might even think that you are "god" by thinking that everything you have is because "you" did it. Not realizing that God put it there for you to have. If God did not create it how could you obtain it? You couldn't because it would be non-existing. Did you create yourself? The answer is no. And if you believe in reincarnation, again who gave you the ability to reincarnate yourself back to earth? Because it wasn't you. Whether you want to acknowledge it, there is a supernatural being that is much greater than you and I. God is a jealous God.

An ungodly soul tie also will prevent you from giving and receiving love and will cause your heart to harden. Please stop justifying these ungodly soul ties because you are caught up. Ungodly Soul Ties must be destroyed. They only produce *death. Is he or she loving you to death or to life?* Or vise - versa. Do you really know what love is? Because it darn sure ain't sleeping with another woman or man because your man asked you to. That's insanity, and I know you are not that desperate for a man or a woman.

Or do you think that love is how many times your dude makes you cum or how many tricks you can do while smashin'? You can do all the tricks in the world—splits, flips, and hang from chandeliers. That will not make a man's heart love you. All you are doing is unnecessary exercise. After all of that, you are still going to feel lonely, empty, tired and possibly sore.

All Sly had to do was tell me what I wanted to hear and that would shut me up. But the reality is that he didn't mean what he was saying. If a man or woman can't keep their promises, you better not give them your heart. *Guard your heart.* Action does speak louder than words.

Love is an action word. Maya Angelou said it best, "When someone shows you who they are, believe them." Anyone can talk a good game. But never forget to do the reference checks. Their character and lifestyle will tell you everything.

Love yourself and your children more and break that bad habit. Single mothers stop putting all of your time and energy in a chump and redirect your energy into your children in a positive way. Stop chasing a man or women and focus on your children. Get your priorities straight. You do not have to deal with drama or negative people in your circle. Your association depicts who you are. "Bad company corrupts good character." Do not listen to unwise family members or so – called friends that say you should "support" a family member or friend's event that goes against your moral standards. Those people do not know how much it took for you to get free. Or how much it takes for you to remain free. "They" do not understand or care because "they" are not free. People who truly love you will not try to pull you down.

The reality is "they" really want you to go back to your old ways. "They" are trying to entice you for their own personal sick gain. This is the true reason why "they" invited you in the first place. Now "they" are mad at you because "they" can't persuade you to go back. Now "they" are calling you "deep, selfish, high sodiety," and only the Lord knows what else. While "they" are talking about you behind your back, God is going to continue to bless you right in front of their faces. If there intentions are genuine, "they" will understand. Individuals with a genuine heart will not want to distract you from God. "They" will respect you and respect the "new" you.

You were made to "stand out" and not fit in. It's a shame that people rather see you at the bottom, because "they" are too lazy to strive to the top.

Who cares! And who cares if "they" talk about you? So what!!! At the beginning and end of the day, what "they" say will not affect the way God blesses you. However, it will affect the way God blesses them. Know That!!! Please God and Not man. True love will find you, but you must wait on it. In the meantime, rekindle the love you have for yourself and reconnect with your children.

First you can begin to humble yourself to your children by being honest and telling them you are sorry for the mistakes you made. Parents we are not perfect. We are human and that includes me and you. And we have human issues. Stop being so prideful because that is not love. Please don't justify your mistakes by not acknowledging them or telling your kids, "I feed you, clothe you and you are well taken care of." You might have done all of these things, but you also did some real hurtful things to your children: Example, lying on your children because of your secret jealousy towards them. Along with causing confusion amongst family members because of your insecurities and wanting family members to choose sides.

Because of your jealously, you do not want anyone in the family to speak good about your child. You buy your child material things, or do certain things out of guilt, obligation or for show. Just so you can throw it up in there face later, along with telling family members what you did.

You exaggerate the truth to make yourself look good. Because of your false accusations concerning your child, you make love one's believe that he or she is ungrateful.

But love had nothing to do with your "guilt gifts" and your child knows this. You show favoritism to your children. *Every opinion about your child is always negative*. Instead of you embracing your child's strength and success, you try to secretly defame it. Or you try to use them. You do not even spend quality time with them. Then your child feels that the only way he or she can connect with you is by allowing you to use them. Because the only time you show them any attention is when you "need" something from them. So they do, and give you what you ask for. But because you are never satisfied you complain. And say, "He or she should have given me more." So you make up lies to try to destroy your child and your child's reputation.

Simply because you are not happy within your own self, due to your own personal deep rooted issues that terrorizes you. "They" side – eyed, lied and killed Jesus. What makes you think that "they" will not try to do the same to you? Just because "they" are "family" does not mean that "they" want the best for you. Sometimes family members and close friends will kick your back in quicker than a stranger. Simply, because "they" are hatin' on you from the sideline. A friend that turns into an enemy always hated on you. "They" started hatin' on you when "they" realized that you were trying to climb out of the crab barrel. Then when you successfully climbed out, "they" really hated you. Check this out Crabs. Keep rolling your eyes and keep talking about me, because I am out the barrel. And I am going to Stay Out because "God will always make my enemies my footstool."

These people are "weak minded" and "they" are intimidated by your strength, success, courage and realness. What "they" do not realize that in your weakness God strength is made perfect and that "No weapon formed against me shall prosper. It will never work."

You over step your boundaries being that you have co-dependency issues and you enjoy contention. You purposely provoke your children to anger because you are envious of their favor and blessings that is bestowed upon them by God. Then you turn around and tell your children "Honor thy Father and Mother for your days will be long." To try to manipulate and control your children because "you" want your child to live the life "you" want them to live. The Bible also states" Father's provoke not your children to wrath." That includes Mother's as well. And because of your fear and control issues all you do is gossip which cause's dissension and discord amongst family members.

Stop trying to make your children miserable because you are. And stop quoting scriptures that you think will fit your controlling and sick needs because of your religious spirit. You have the audacity to say to your child "the only reason why you are blessed is because of "you." Your child is "blessed" because of his/her love, obedience, suffering, faith and relationship with God. Instead of you giving God the Glory, you give yourself the "glory."

Not realizing or caring that your child almost "lost their mind" because of your wickedness. Parents practice what you preach and stop acting like you were born perfect. Stop gossiping. Pray for yourself first and deal with your insecure issues and then you will be able to pray for your children effectively. Maybe then you will see positive results. You tell people that your child is "disrespectful." Because you're adult child disagrees with your negative opinions and actions. And he / she will not allow you to control them anymore. Your adult child is not four but almost forty, he / she has the right to have their own positive opinion and just because he / she does not agree with you does not mean that they are being disrespectful.

Parents you must realize that you are not always right. We are still human. And just because we did something's a certain way did not mean it was right. But because you are stuck in your ways, you tell your adult child "We've been doing this for this long and we are not going to change." This is the reason why your adult child does not come around you. Negative opinions is dead unnecessary weight that your adult child does not have to subject there self to. Life alone is hard enough. Your adult child is aware of where your negativity got you. Which is bitter, angry, stagnate, sick, miserable and living in a world called "facade." Trying to make your "façade" your "reality." So as a result, your child desires a non – toxic life. And when you give your adult child advice out of fear and your adult child has faith, you and your child will never see eye to eye. Or vise-versa. People that have faith think completely different from people who have fear. Faith will keep you free. Fear will keep you stuck.

And the reality is some of your adult children have more faith than you ever had. Somewhere along the line, parents you lost your faith due to you experiencing so many disappointments. Get your faith back. God never disappoints. People do. The streets say in order to get respect you have to give it. I disagree. In order to get respect you have to respect yourself first. How can you respect someone else if you do not respect yourself? Respect does not speak negative or have a negative motive attached to it. Maybe if you get free, respect your child's adult hood and stop speaking negative about them and to them. Maybe you and your child would have a relationship. Something to think about parents.

Parents aren't we supposed to live by example? You can't sow seeds of dishonor in your child's life or anyone's life and think in return God will honor you. When you truly love and honor someone, you will always see the best in them and not the worst. The truth is, "you" only see the worst in people, when you are jealous of their best.

God only elevates individuals that operate in pure honor. Control is not love. Control is witchcraft. It's all or nothing when it comes to the Word of God. Everyone has a part and must do their part. The Bible is not one sided. God is LOVE not lies, drama, pride, control, confusion, envy, fear, constant misunderstandings or judging others. Be honest with yourself and admit that you did this to your children. Tell your kids you are sorry, and mean it. Stop acting like your children do not know what's going on because they do know.

Okay, children your parents may never admit to you that

they wronged you because of pride. Love, pray, forgive and respect them anyway. It will be hard but you MUST. You might just have to eat the meat and spit out the bones. Let it go. Move on, be positive and live your life. Don't let un-forgiveness block your blessings because un-forgiveness will. Learn from their mistakes and do not repeat the cycle. God chose you to break the chain because you have strong faith. God loves you and I promise you, he will heal you and take great care of you. God knows the truth and that is all that matters. God got you. Smile! Move Forward. "When my father and mother forsake me, then the LORD will take me up." That's a promise from God. Enjoy your life with character and integrity. Remember God is a good God even on a bad day.

Mother's /single mother's we must do better, our kids are the future. Stop putting a man before your kids because you're desperate. Stop being so thirsty! Get your mind right and heal! So when Mr. Right gets here, you will be able to recognize, love and appreciate him. You won't be trippin' on him because you never got over your last lying, cheating, and abusive relationship. And if you are in an abusive relationship leave him or her alone.

Mother's stop blaming your "no good" baby father's for your child's troubled behaviors. Everything is not your child's father's fault. Remember mother's you slept with him and had a baby for him. So what does that make you? You are attracted to what is inside of you. You produce after your own kind. Take responsibility for your own actions. It's tight but it's right.

Fathers now I'm coming for you, stop telling your children empty promises and getting their hopes up. You tell your children that you are going to pick them up and never come. Your child waits for you for hours because they believe in you. You never show up or call them to let them know you are not coming.

Father's when you tell your children you are going to do something for them. Dog on it. Do it! Stop blaming their mothers. Their mothers had nothing to do with you not doing what you are supposed to do for your children. Take responsibility. What type of man has pride and do not take care of their kids?

In the working world, no calls and no shows are grounds for termination. And you wonder why your children are not feeling you. How can they? Now the mothers have to redirect a hurt and angry child. When your child is calling you from their phone you don't pick up. But when the mother calls you from her phone the bizarre thing is you answer. As a result the mother tells you off and then you have the nerve to say to your child's mother.

"You are just mad because I don't want you." News flash! Boo-boo! "She-don't-want-you," however she does want you to help her with the child. Notice I wrote help and not hurt the child.

Stop trying to flatter yourself. You are no longer important to her. Your child's mother grew up and all the way out of you. The only person that still loves you and has hope in your lying behind is your child. Us mature mothers are trying really hard to encourage our children to still love and respect you in spite of your irresponsible actions.

Real women are not turned on by a man that does not take care of his kids. We are turned off. The truth is you are angry because your child's mom been stop sleeping with you and has moved on. And because you know you no longer have control over your child's mother emotions. You try to control her emotions by hurting her through the child. Grow up! You are half of hundred. Your immature tactics are not working. By Boy! Now Digest that.

Everyone needs to find out who they are in Christ quick. Because this "craziness" is universal and it must Stop! Children don't deserve to be hurt by their parents.

Satan is cheap and he will allow you to allow people to treat you like garbage. You are a child of the King the most High and True and Living God. **The Creator of All.**

Stop thinking of sex as just a physical act because it is not, it's spiritual to. Just like faith and prayer is spiritual or should I say, "at times an unseen act." But when done you will receive and experience great results. When you smash you don't see at first that he or she is crazy, has a STD, hurt, drama, empty promises, emotional turmoil, mental anguish, unnecessary crying spells, unwanted pregnancy and future heart break.

But eventually you will see these entire things manifest because what you sow in your flesh you will definitely reap.

There is no good thing that dwells in your flesh. Don't be deceived, lust will fool you because it feels good but the consequences are major. Everything that looks, feels, and taste good to you is not always good for you. Some people and something's are just "no good" for you. Stop touching the unclean thing. Stop hiding behind your mask of hurt, fear, insecurities and a broken heart.

Take that stupid mask off and be honest with yourself and get free.

I know you're saying there is a lack of men. But with God, there is no lack. God lacks nothing because he is God. Don't ever get that twisted. All you need is one penis because you have one vagina. *You don't need no extras.* However, if you do have extra's. God loves you and so do I. Only God can judge you. Know That!

Some people label me as being brutally honest; however, I consider myself usefully honest. Reason being that my honesty comes from a genuine place. A place wanting you to be better and to feel better about yourself.

Useful honesty clears away lies and exposes dark places. How can you heal if you keep hiding?

And once you stop hiding, how can you heal if you keep going back to what or who is hurting you? You can't! Stop going back. Do not go back to your past because you are having problems in your present. Persevere and keep moving forward. God does reward obedience and your faith pleases him.

Some resentful people try to defame those who shine light into dark places and try to turn and twist your words by being cunning and manipulating. Oftentimes, usefully honest people are misunderstood because we speak up even when it's difficult and because of our God-given boldness. We are not stunted by rules of etiquette.

Watch out for people who always tell you what you want to hear because most manipulators will use such tact to manipulate you right out of your thongs, draws, and money. Hello somebody.

Ask God to allow you to discern people's hearts and spirits because a lot of people talk out of both sides of their neck. I'd rather be called usefully honest than a practiced liar.

If people can't handle the truth, that's on them, not you.

However, there is a time to keep silent and a time to speak. In your time of silence, watch—I repeat, watch—as well as pray. I have no tolerance for nonsense. In your time of speaking, nip it in the bud. But if foolish people don't get it, say no more. Continue to pray and go on with your life. Don't live life like you are broken. Every action does not have to have a *negative reaction*.

Sometimes you might have to walk away and never look back.

Forgive yourself and those who hurt you.

There is so much power in love and forgiveness. The Bible instructs us to "love our enemies, not trust our enemies."

Trust is earned.

That includes parents, spouses, baby fathers, baby mothers, family members, so-called friends, church members, co-workers and even your dog.

When your dog turns on you; you put the dog to sleep. Well it's time, for you to put some people to sleep. Without bad blood.

Everything happens for a reason. You must let the hurt go so you can heal correctly and effectively fulfill the purpose God has for you.

If you do not know your purpose, just ask God, and he will reveal it to you. In the meantime, be still and know that God is God. When you learn how to get to the heart of God, he will then open up his hands.

Be totally free because who the son sets free is free indeed. You are fearfully and wonderfully made. Your soul knows it and now you do.

No matter what wrong or right you do, always run to God and not away from him.

Be mindful, for the wages of sin is death, but the gift of God is eternal life through Jesus Christ our Lord.

God is here to help you because he loves you.

Sometimes you have to darn near lose your mind to get the "mind of Christ."

And almost lose your life to "find your life through Christ Jesus." Selah.

Do God, not you or people, because that's what separates the grown women from the girls and the men from the boys.

Nobody wants you blessed like God. The devil thought he had me, but I got away. And so will you!

"HE TURNED IT." That song by Tye Tribbett is the truth.

God gave me beauty instead of ashes and he will do the same for you, if you allow him to do so.

If you need to know the plan for your life, get in the spirit and let the Lord minister to you.

This message has been approved by God. To God be the glory!

What the devil meant for evil. God will turn it around for your good.

Trust him! You trusted everyone else now it's time for you to Trust God.

Beloved, I pray that in all respects you may prosper and be in good health just as your soul prospers.

—3 John 1:2

Amen.

From a healed soul to another,

Twinkle

PS: Whatever you do, don't lose your relationship with Jesus. Now walk in Freedom and Victory!!!

Discussion Questions

1. Who is your favorite character? And Why?

2. What chapter did you relate to the most?

3. Why do you think it took Twinkle so long to leave Sly?

4. Do you think that there was ever a time that Sly loved Twinkle?

5. Do you think that Twinkle could have left Sly without a change mind set?

6. Do you feel that you are Ungodly Soul Tied to someone?

7. If you have an Ungodly Soul Tie. Are you taking the necessary steps to destroy it?

8. Or do you even want the Ungodly Soul Tie destroyed? Just being real.

9. Do you believe that where you're going in life will be better than where you been?

10. If so, break the Ungodly Soul Tie. You have no more time to waste. Move forward.

11. You can do it! It's your time! ☺

Made in the USA
Charleston, SC
27 October 2014